PRIVATE CATHAY'S SECRET

By

Rebecca O. Hayes

SCROLL BOOKS

ISBN: 1456306030
EAN – 13   9781456306038

Library of Congress Control Number 2010919199

This book is a work of historical fiction. Names, characters,
places, and incidents are based on actual events.
Bibliographical references are included.

Place orders at:
www.rebeccawords4all.com

ACKNOWLEDGMENTS

I am extremely grateful to those persons who made this telling of Cathay Williams' story possible. Although I have fictionalized her story in Private Cathay's Secret, it is based on many realistic facts, regions and situations in her life. In order to make Cathay's story come alive, I submitted it to a number of people for critiques. I must acknowledge the members of the Scottsdale, AZ Adult and Children's Writers groups, especially Deborah Ledford who continually encouraged and mentored me in format and submitting style. Thanks to SCBWI-AZ with their regional advisor, Michelle Parker-Rock, and to the Highlights Chautauqua Writing Workshop who launched me into Children's writing.

Also, thanks go to my teacher friends, Corliss Pearson and Flora Eikerenkoetter, and to my middle grade readers, Cameron McDaniel and Sydney Larrier, for their insights on what would make the story more interesting for young people. To Pamela and Joel Tuck, I give my heartfelt gratitude for sharing their publishing wisdom. With their help I am able to bring Cathay's story to light.

Finally, I am most appreciative to my husband, Roland Hayes, who brought the story of Cathay Williams to my attention. He guided me in researching the facts of her life, and provided information about the Buffalo Soldiers and the military terms I used when telling the story. His constant reassurance and support has been my mainstay throughout.

Rebecca O. Hayes

PRIVATE CATHAY'S SECRET

Prologue
St. Louis, Missouri, 1866

Cathay Williams stood outside the St. Louis courthouse for a long time. She looked down at the baggy pants and blousy shirt she was wearing, clothes found in Miz Powers' washhouse. Her pants were held up by cord suspenders across the shoulders, and the shirt flapped in the gentle breeze that blew across the square. *These don't half fit me none,* she thought, *but maybe they do the trick.* Cathay brushed her large, calloused hands over her head of short, wooly hair as she stared at the former slaves lined up beside her. Would the U.S. Army really take these men to join up like her cousin Jasper said? Some of them wore ill-fitting faded blue or gray uniforms, mostly ragged. Others wore dusty overalls and shirts with patches on top of patches such as those they had worn in the fields. Still others were dressed much as she was. Cathay watched the men in the line press forward toward the recruitment table.

A uniformed soldier approached and slapped her shoulder. "Go on fella," he said. "If you gonna join up, you'd better get in line. After awhile they're gonna stop you colored boys from signing up."

A smile creased Cathay Williams' face.

The would-be recruit chuckled and thought, *that soldier thinks I'm a man.*

PART ONE
JOHNSON PLANTATION, OUTSIDE
JEFFERSON CITY, MISSOURI
EARLY 1861

CHAPTER 1

Cathay Williams crept quietly into Master Joseph's room and closed the door. She laid an armful of linens on the thick four poster bed and pretended to feather dust the ornately carved mahogany wardrobe that stood beside it. Although Cathay despised the house duties that Mama gave her, duties of dusting, washing, mending, and helping in the kitchen, she never minded taking the laundry up to Master Joseph's room. The manliness of the room, the tobacco smell, and the rich earthy colors of the walls, rugs and bed coverings gave her a sense of strength and power whenever she entered.

Cathay knew she would provoke Mama if she lingered there too long, but she couldn't resist admiring the elaborate scene on the massive mahogany table in front of the tall double windows. A felt cloth covering made the table resemble a grassy battleground with its rows of little military figures, lined up for battle. She peered at some of the soldiers placed behind miniature cannons on the felt covered table top; some standing with their guns pointed; others kneeling, rifles balanced on one knee.

Martha, Cathay's mama and the Johnson's cook, wanted to groom Cathay as a house servant, especially to help her in the kitchen, but Cathay didn't want to learn to cook. Sixteen-year-old Cathay had heard of war being talked about. The military nature of Master Joseph's bedroom fascinated her and she imagined herself as one of the little men in uniform.

She'd heard the tales of regiments of soldiers gathering to fight for the Confederacy, tales brought by slaves that came from nearby Independence. Even though she knew she was a slave, she wished she could be a soldier. It seemed like that would be an exciting life.

Cathay scanned the imitation battlefield, noting the position each soldier held. Oh, how she wanted to handle the tiny figures! They drew her tall, muscular body to them like a bear to a hive of bees. Cathay took a deep breath. Slowly, she reached a long, pointed finger toward the glistening canon. As she touched the cool metal surface, a sharp voice split the air.

"What do you think you're doing?"

Cathay jumped at the sound.

Master Joseph had opened the door so quietly that Cathay never heard him creep behind.   Startled, her elbow hit the table. One hand brushed the cannon and swept it into the rows of soldiers. The other hand holding the feather duster flew to her mouth. Feathers and dust floated into her face. She sneezed.

"Achoo. S-sorry, Mastah Joe." Cathay gasped. "I was just trying to find a way to d-dust." Cathay trembled as she saw Master Joseph's angry expression. His eyes were cold slits of gray steel as he raised his hand to swat her. Instead he yelled.

"Get out of here and don't you ever come in here again."

Cathay dropped the feather duster and stumbled from the room. Forgetting the linens she was supposed to put away, she flew downstairs.

* * *

Cathay's mama spooned batter for dumplings into a pot of chicken stew. As Cathay ran trembling into the kitchen, she faced her mama's glare.

"You was supposed to be here long before now, Missy. Where you been?"

"Uh-I-uh-I was-uh..." she began. She cringed.

"What's wrong with you, Cathay Williams? What you done, gal?"

Cathay's eyes widened and filled with tears. She knew her mama would get into trouble along with her if the young master told his father.

Cathay couldn't tell Mama about knocking the soldiers over. Not the whole truth.

"I was upstairs putting away the linen in Mastah Joe's room. While I was dusting, Mastah Joe's soldiers fell over. He yelled at me."

As Cathay watched Mama's lips tighten, she realized she was in big trouble. She saw Mama's eyes close to slits and her nose flared.

"So they just fell over all by theyselves, huh?" Martha pushed Cathay toward the kitchen door. "You better get on down to the quarters and help Miz Alice with her chil'ren." she said. "I'm-a take care you later."

Cathay hurried from the kitchen and down the road to the slave quarters. When Mama threatened with her lips tight like that, Cathay knew she was sure in for a good whipping.

CHAPTER 2

"**Y**ou knows I sure do appreciate you helping keep these chil'ren busy and out-a my hair," said Miz Alice as she sat on her stoop shelling peas into the apron spread on her lap.

Cathay didn't mind helping Miz Alice with her eight children, ages three months to eight years. The cabin was next door to Cathay's, and Mama helped Miz Alice whenever she could.

"Yes'm. I know. They be sent to the fields soon enough," Cathay answered. "'Specially Lucy and Luke.

They getting pretty big. And the others move more'n a passel-a crickets in summer." She looked over at the children running around, in and out of the bushes and under and over the stoop where Miz Alice sat. She knew the overseer would soon be sending for Miz Alice's eight-year-old twins, to help out in the fields. Cathay enjoyed giving them as much play time as she could before that happened.

"You know how much I hates being with Mama in that kitchen. I rather be with your chil'ren. At least it means I can be out in the fresh air having fun."

If not for the threat of a whipping hanging over her head, Cathay would have welcomed escaping to be with Miz Alice.

Later, Cathay rounded up the children and helped give them supper. After she sent them to bed, she sat by the dusty road waiting for Mama to come down from the big house. She watched Miz Alice back on the stoop rocking and humming to Baby Hosea while she nursed him. She heard the rocker squeaking a rhythmic lullaby as Miz Alice's plump body moved back and forth.

While she waited, Cathay traced lines in the dust with a stick and worried. *Wonder what Mama's gonna do to me when she gets home.*

Mama often brought home left over vittles from the master's supper for Cathay and her cousin, Jasper, who stayed with them. "Prob'ly won't get nothin' tonight," Cathay said to herself. She could feel her stomach grumbling, partly from hunger, partly from fear. She knew Mama was really mad at her for meddling in the young master's room. Jasper would probably get all of whatever Mama brought home.

I be lucky if I get any grits, fatback, and cornbread we usually eat for supper. I probably should-a ate with Miz Alice's chil'ren. Mama'll likely send me to bed without no supper.

Cathay hated that Mama always spoiled Jasper. He was Mama's nephew, her sister's boy. When Mama's sister died from the coughing sickness, Mama had promised she would take care of him. She always said Jasper was a growing boy and needed all the food they could spare. Sometimes Cathay wished Old Master William Johnson, Joseph's father, would have sold Jasper away when Mama's sister died. Often that happened to other families during slavery. When families weren't complete, the odd members got sold to other plantations.

Suddenly a gong sounded.

Cathay knew all the slaves were being summoned to the big house for something important. She saw Jasper run up to the road from the stable where he helped tend the horses.

"Come on," he called to Cathay. He and Cathay bounded up the hill. Other slaves poured out of their shacks, or were returning from the fields. On the way, they met Mama carrying a bundle she'd salvaged from the kitchen.

"What's the gong for, Auntie?" asked Jasper.

"I don't rightly know, but you best get up there and find out. Run on. I be along directly."

They ran ahead, but Cathay turned around once and saw her mama trudge wearily down to the quarters.

* * *

The slaves gathered on the expanse of lawn around the circular veranda of the plantation house. Mingling with the others, Jasper and Cathay heard snatches of conversation.

"What you think Mastah want?"

"What's happnin' we gotta come up here?"

"Must be somethin' awful important 'cause I'm near 'bout dead tired."

The murmuring of voices gradually died down as young Master Joseph helped his father's squat frame across the veranda. Severely overweight and wheezing badly, Master William leaned heavily on the veranda railing. The old Master spoke in a quavering voice.

"Yankees are stirring up trouble for the South," he announced. "President Davis and the militia are asking for soldiers. My son, Joseph, is going to join up with the Missouri regiment in Independence. He'll take whatever weapons we have here with him. You all find other ways to protect our land if need be. Remember, this is your home and you have to fight to stay here. Those Yankees'll take you and sell you far away from here if you don't defend this place. You know you don't want that."

A fearful murmur spread through the group of slaves listening to this grave announcement. The threat of being sold or captured hung in the air. Master William threw his hand in the air to dismiss everyone and limped back across the veranda and into the house. Master Joseph followed.

Cathay's mishap with the tin soldiers did not seem important anymore.

CHAPTER 3

The weeks stretched into months. Life on the plantation continued as usual. The field workers tended the hemp crop supervised by Jim Long, the Johnson's overseer. He brought news of the war from Jefferson City from time to time, but no one knew where Master Joseph was.

Cathay continued to work in the big house, but did not visit Master Joseph's room anymore. Since she'd escaped a whipping once, she wasn't willing to chance it another time.

One night, as Cathay tried to wait up for Mama to come down to their cabin in the quarters, her eyes became heavy. She fell asleep curled up in a ball on the floor by the dead embers of the fireplace. She was still sleeping when the first rays of sunlight crept across the fields, and Jasper came into the cabin from the stable where he'd slept.

"Where's Auntie?" he asked, as he prodded Cathay awake with his toe.

Cathay squirmed, rubbed her eyes, and sat up. "She didn't come home last night," she said.

Jasper pushed her harder with his foot. "You better get up that big house and see why."

Cathay knew Jasper loved to give her orders when Mama wasn't around. Usually Cathay would cuff him on the arm or give him a smart answer. But she was too groggy this time. She crawled up and hobbled off to the yard in back of the cabin where the rain barrel stayed. Stiff from sleeping on the hard earthen floor with its woven straw covering, Cathay flexed her arms and shrugged her shoulders, trying to loosen up. She dipped some rain water from the barrel into a nearby bowl.

"Brrrr." Cathay shivered as she splashed the cold water on her face with her hands.

Only slightly refreshed, Cathay started up the road to the plantation house. The air was crisp and the ground wet from the early morning dew. Sorry she had not thought to put a wrap around her shoulders, Cathay hugged herself, rubbed her arms briskly to warm them, and trotted up the hill.

She wondered what could have kept Mama from returning home her usual time. Cathay's pace quickened as she approached the kitchen door. The early morning stiffness was almost gone when she entered the room. There was no lively fire her mama usually made to cook breakfast, although a few coals still glowed in the fireplace. Neither did there seem to be any food laid out in readiness.

Cathay tiptoed toward the front of the house and listened for sounds of movement. She heard muffled voices coming from the upstairs hallway as she started to climb the stairs. She watched her mama come out of the old master's room carrying a basin and towels. Usually perky and jolly, Tazzie, the upstairs maid, looked tearful as she followed Mama with a basket of soiled linens. Her face matched Mama's; solemn and downcast..

As Mama and Tazzie descended, Cathay backed down the stairs. They all headed toward the kitchen and out the door in silence. Cathay's mama gave the towels to Tazzie who slipped quietly off to the washhouse.

"Old Mastah died last night," Mama whispered. "We been up cleaning him and that bedroom. Getting him ready to be laid out."

Cathay watched her mama dump the water from the basin on the ground behind the garden. She then continued to the washhouse where she left the basin with Tazzie. Cathay stood in the yard and waited for her mama to bring fresh water. Together they returned to the kitchen.

"Don't know what's gonna become-a us," Mama said softly, shaking her head. "Miz Elizabeth a widow now Old Mastah's gone. We just have to help her all we can, I reckon."

* * *

With that, she began bustling around the fireplace, stirring the few red embers into life, readying the fire to cook the morning meal.

CHAPTER 4

Six more months went by. Cathay continued working in the big house, but hated every minute of it. She wondered how Tazzie could perform her duties in the house with so much gaiety, always singing and laughing. Cathay retreated to the back of the big house whenever she could, with the pretense of helping Reuben in the garden. Mama would eventually spot her and make her come inside.

One day, while outside, she saw a buckboard and horse arriving at the front of the house.

Cathay ran inside and called up the staircase. "Miz Elizabeth, there some people rolled up in the yard." Her mistress ran down the stairs and out the door. Martha, Cathay, and Tazzie followed close behind.

Cathay watched a thin, pale woman climb down from the buckboard into Elizabeth Johnson's embrace. The woman bore a strong resemblance to Miz Elizabeth. Her clothes were dusty and disheveled, and her bonnet had slipped from her straw colored hair that was tinged with gray. The bonnet hung haphazardly against the side of her neck. Cathay watched as Elizabeth hugged her sister tightly.

"Oh, Laura, we were so worried about you when we heard about the fire around Phelps County," she cried. "We didn't know if you survived or not."

"I would be dead if my groom, Jonah, hadn't sneaked me away. We headed across the pasture in the buckboard to the back road just as those soldiers set fire to the house," said Laura.

As Jonah sat quietly holding the horse's reins, Cathay wondered what caused all the excitement.

Elizabeth called, "Martha, come get Miss Laura's things. Cathay, run tell Homer to come help Jonah put the horse away. Then you take Miss Laura's things up to the spare bedroom. Tazzie can make it ready while Martha gives her something to eat. Then she can go up and rest." With her arms around Laura's frail shoulders, Elizabeth led her sister into the house.

Beckoning Jonah to drive the horse toward the stable, Cathay gave Elizabeth's message to Homer, the Johnson's groom. She skipped around, excitedly asking Jonah questions.

"Where you come from, Jonah? What kind of fire is Miz Elizabeth talking about? Was they Yankees burning Miz Laura's house? Where you think they gonna go next?"

Jonah gave Cathay a half smile, shook his head, and tried to answer her rapid fire questions. "Them Union soldiers come from around Fort Rolla. They burnt up all the farms near about Phelps County. First they stole all they could. Then they set fire to Miz Laura's house. We barely got away before they would-a caught us."

With a gasp, Cathay's mouth dropped open in astonishment and her eyes widened.

"You think they gonna be coming here next? They gonna burn us out too?"

"Don't know. They's a good piece away so far," Jonah said as he and Homer unharnessed the horse and led it into the stable. "We just gotta be on the lookout for them."

After putting Miz Laura's things in the spare room, Cathay headed back downstairs. As she passed the dining room, she heard Elizabeth and Laura talking.

"I wouldn't be here today if it wasn't for Jonah. It sure is good to have faithful servants. Make sure he gets some supper. He must be plumb tired. I know I am." Laura paused and took a deep breath. "That food sure smells good. I think I could eat a horse."

"Shall I tell Homer to shoot yours?" joked Elizabeth, trying to cheer up her sister.

"My lands, no." Laura chuckled. "I'll settle for what you got Martha fixing."

Before she got caught eavesdropping, Cathay hurried to her mama, so she didn't hear any more. She helped Mama warm over the evening meal of biscuits, rice, snap beans, and smothered chicken in gravy. She then went to put out serving dishes and plates in the dining room.

When she entered to set the table, Cathay saw Miz Elizabeth with her head in her hands. As she looked up, Cathay could see she had been crying. She frowned and her mouth quivered as she related the latest news to her sister.

"We haven't heard from Joseph but twice since he left. We got a letter when he first enlisted and another when he transferred to Georgia. That was months and months ago. No word since then. He doesn't even know about William's death."

Cathay stood by the door as the sisters continued their conversation.

"You know the Yankees are getting closer." Laura leaned toward Elizabeth and lowered her voice. "If I hadn't sewed my money in my clothes earlier, I wouldn't have had anything when Jonah drove me away. What those Yankees didn't steal, they burned. We bribed the ferry driver to take us across the Maries River."

Cathay wanted to hear more, but just then her mama called her.

That night Cathay told her mama what she'd overheard.

"Unnh-unh," Mama grunted. She sucked her teeth and shook her head. "That's gonna mean more work for us."

* * *

The next day Elizabeth called Martha, Tazzie, and Cathay together in Laura's bedroom and told her what they planned to do.

"Tazzie, you and Cathay get busy and cut open the mattresses and the hems of our clothes. We'll hide the silver in the bedding and money and jewelry in our clothes, especially our underwear. Martha, you help us sew the seams back together."

Laura looked around. "If soldiers come, they will no doubt be looking for things they can sell. Anything around of value?"

"I suppose some of Joseph's books and tin soldiers might sell," said Elizabeth. "If we tell the Yankees about Joseph's room, they might rummage through it and leave the rest of the house alone."

Cathay hated going to the old master's room, because the stench of urine and feces from the master's diseased body still remained in the room. William Johnson's body had become dried and wrinkled and rank during the time he was ill. Even though the servants had washed the smelly linens, the door and drapes had stayed closed ever since his death. So Martha sent Cathay with Tazzie to take out the hems from the clothing in the other bedrooms.

When Cathay thought of the elaborate tin soldier collection Master Joseph had in his room, she jumped at the chance to help Tazzie upstairs.

"We better go get those clothes," said Tazzie. "I show you how you get out the hems."

They worked long hours opening seams and hiding precious belongings into hems. They stuffed bulky silver items into mattresses, securing them from the Yankees.

One day, when Tazzie wasn't looking, Cathay entered young Master Joseph's room. It was still untouched, just as Joseph had left it. She tiptoed over to the felt covered table and stared at the miniature battlefield. Cathay threw her shoulders back and flexed her arm muscles in what she imagined was a military manner. Then, ever so gently, she lifted the kneeling soldier from its spot and dropped it into her apron pocket. As she heard Tazzie's footsteps approach, she hurried from the room. That was the last time she risked a look at Master Joseph's play battlefield, hoping the figure would not be missed if the Yankees took the tin soldiers.

* * *

Day by day the women waited for news from Joseph Johnson. Nobody knew where he was or whether he was alive or dead.

CHAPTER 5

Cathay ducked out the kitchen door when she saw Jim Long galloping toward the house. Mama had told her to stay out of sight whenever he came around. Mama told Cathay the wily overseer would put her in the field if he had a chance. She knew Long was cruel because he had worked the field and stable hands unmercifully since the old master's death. She had already helped Mama treat Jasper's scathed back from a whipping he'd gotten. Jasper had given Long some back talk about something he knew wasn't right concerning the horses. Mama said bold, outspoken Cathay would suffer the same fate if she and

Long had any argument. Best she stay away when he came to the big house.

*   *   *

Long had already asked Elizabeth to send him some of the house servants to help in the field at hemp and tobacco harvest time. Only Martha, Tazzie, Cathay, and Reuben, the gardener, were left. Martha knew it wouldn't be long before he recognized how tall and muscular Cathay had become.

As Cathay grew older, she'd grown taller and looked strong enough to work in the fields. By now she was eighteen and Mama had caught Jim Long staring at her daughter in a vulgar way. Often the overseers would take advantage of young slave girls against their will. That's when Mama told Cathay to make herself scarce when Long came to the house. Martha begged Miz Elizabeth to let Cathay stay with the house staff to help in the kitchen. That way she would stay out of Jim Long's sight and attention.

Actually, Cathay wanted to leave the domestic work in the big house and work in the fields and stables. She preferred being outdoors with the sun on her face and the wind blowing through her corn-rowed hair, even if the work was hard. She liked being with the horses, too. But she didn't relish the idea of being whipped if she sassed the overseer like Jasper did. Or getting any other kind of treatment or punishment Jim Long decided to give her. She knew when Old Mastah was alive, he wouldn't allow his slaves to be beaten. But Miz Elizabeth was afraid of Long. Mama said Cathay would have to go to the fields if the overseer insisted.

Cathay crept around the side of the house and stooped beneath the veranda. She saw Long, looking down from his horse at Miz Elizabeth standing at the end of the walkway. Cathay couldn't hear what he was saying, but she heard him snarl as he threw an envelope at Miz Elizabeth. As Elizabeth bent to pick up the envelope, Long spurred his horse and pulled back on the reins spraying sand and dust in the air. The horse reared as Jim Long laughed and galloped away.

Miz Elizabeth shuddered and Cathay saw her shoulders slump. Shaking sand from her hair and brushing the dust from her dress, Miz Elizabeth turned and trudged back to the house.

Cathay felt sorry for her. Mama said the field hands had told her that ever since Old Master got sick, Long had been stealing money whenever he sold crops from the plantation.

Still Miz Elizabeth managed to keep the household running. She also managed to keep her faithful house servants, but none of them knew how long it would be before the war would change things.

CHAPTER 6

Heavy hoof beats pounded near the Johnson Plantation. Cathay looked up from shucking corn in the yard by the kitchen door. The sound came from the road leading to the big house. She wondered if the Yankee soldiers had finally come.

As the hoof beats got louder, Cathay dropped her pan, and, stepping over the corn that scattered on the ground, ran into the house.

"Mama, Mama. There's horses coming up the road. Sounds like lots-a horses."

Martha wiped her hands on her apron and gave Cathay a shove. "Run upstairs and tell Miz Elizabeth. Hurry, gal."

Cathay ran.

Martha removed the kettle from the fire and looked around the kitchen before she hurried to the front of the house.

Elizabeth and Laura rushed downstairs. Cathay and Tazzie trailed behind and huddled with Martha near the front door.

Mounted soldiers approached. A platoon of blue uniformed men followed on foot. Some carried rifles. Some carried muskets. All had side arms.

Cathay stood awed by the parade of armed men. She remembered the tin soldiers that Master Joseph kept on the table in his room. But this was a *real* army with *real* guns. Cathay tingled with a mixture of excitement, fear, and expectation. She fingered the tin soldier she always kept secreted in her apron pocket. Something was about to happen, but she didn't know what.

The mounted soldiers galloped up the walkway. Horses' hooves dislodged the sod and some of them trampled the last of Elizabeth's fading flowers. Cathay peered around her mama as one of the riders dismounted and strode up the steps to the front door. Gold braid adorned the soldier's hat and shoulders. A long sword hung at his side. He raised his gloved hand and pounded on the door.

Cathay glanced at her mistress' stern face as she opened the door a few inches.

"Morning, ma'am," greeted the Union officer, nodding. The braid on his uniform glistened in the morning sunlight. The officer smiled at Elizabeth and tipped his hat to put her at ease.

"I'm Colonel William Benton of the 13th Union Army regiment and these are my men. We're here to collect supplies and we need to take some of your farm hands to serve us on our way to Little Rock, Arkansas. We mean you no harm if we can deal with you and your people peaceably."

Elizabeth opened the door a bit more and straightened her back. Though she answered through trembling lips, her azure eyes flashed. "We have little that has not already been stolen," she said. "The only hands left are my overseer and a few old tired servants who work the fields. And of course my house staff."

Cathay saw the soldier turn and scan the sagging veranda, the wasted grounds, and the dying flower garden.

He turned to the soldiers nearby. "You men go inspect the slave quarters for workers and the stables and fields for anybody and anything you think we can use," he ordered. Then he turned back to Elizabeth.

"We want anything you have that we can use or sell, ma'am," he said. "We need supplies. I'll ask your overseer to select some of your slaves to go with us. See what you can collect by the time we return."

With that he tipped his hat, mounted his horse, and rode away.

* * *

The servants all began to talk at once. "What we gonna do, Miz Elizabeth? We ain't hardly got enough for ourselves. Think they gonna burn our house like they did Miz Laura's?"

They followed Elizabeth as she strode toward the kitchen. She lifted her chin, her expression set with determination. "We'll just give these men the least we can find," she said. She paused. Then she continued thoughtfully. "They needn't know about the food in the underground storage bins. They won't search if we give them a few things from the house and the garden and the smokehouse. We'll beg them to leave us enough in the pantry for ourselves. If we cooperate they may not harm us."

Turning to Cathay she ordered, "Cathay, you go help Reuben gather some vegetables from the garden. Then get some meat from the smokehouse. Martha, you and Tazzie come with me." Elizabeth and Laura led the way through the house in search of items that would appease the soldiers.

Cathay found Reuben, who usually tended the house garden the best he could with gnarled hands on aching knees. He always bent over with rheumatism, and snowy beads of fuzz partly covered his shiny brown head. Reuben had hidden in the washhouse when the soldiers approached. He was trembling with fright. Deep trails of worry criss-crossed his aged face as Cathay tried to calm him.

"It's alright, Reuben. I'm-a help you get the food together. Those soldiers don't want no broke down folks like us. They just want vittles."

She helped him gather cabbages, potatoes, onions and pole beans in a sack. Then they went to the smokehouse and hoisted what bacon and meager meat supplies were there from the shelves. They carried the sacks of food around to the front of the house and placed them on the veranda.

A few hours later, Cathay heard a tremulous whinny heralding the Colonel's return. She saw Jim Long riding along with him and some of the slaves who worked the fields, following on foot. With them walked Jasper's friend, Henry. Cathay was surprised to see her cousin with them also. She knew Jasper usually helped Homer in the stables. The colonel had sought out the overseer to help him round up able-bodied men to send to Arkansas.

Elizabeth greeted them as she stood with Laura and the house servants on the veranda.

"We've gathered some food from our garden and smokehouse," she said to the colonel. She pointed to the sack containing the meat and produce. "We've collected candles and candleholders and you're welcome to search our house for anything else you think you can sell."

Cathay knew there was little else that the soldiers could find since her mistress and the rest of the servants had hidden everything of value.

"We've also collected some quilts and pillows and towels so your soldiers can rest warm and comfortable," Elizabeth added sweetly, hoping she could discourage the soldiers from ransacking the house.

Cathay watched Long push his horse forward in front of the colonel. She figured he did not intend for Elizabeth to ignore him as her overseer. He scowled as he leaned down from his horse, and waved his arm toward the group of slaves he brought with him.

"These the boys I'm gonna send with the soldiers," he said. "I can make do with old Hildy and that feebleminded son of hers. I'm keeping Alice's twins and the pale-faced boy with the white eyes too. You'll have to spare Reuben to help Homer and Miz Laura's Jonah with the livestock that's left."

He stared at Martha.

"Oh, yeah," he taunted, "the colonel here wants a cook. Guess you'll have to send Martha with them." He hawked and spewed a stream of brown spittle to the ground. He grinned showing a row of crooked, yellowed teeth.

Cathay gulped. *What was he thinking? How would Mama be able to survive in an army camp?* She watched as her mama folded her arms across her chest and set her jaw firmly. Martha glared at Jim Long. Her eyes narrowed to slits and her lips tightened. Elizabeth's hands flew to her mouth and gasped. Cathay understood how much the household relied on her mama for more things than cooking. If Reuben had to help in the stables, Martha could tend the garden and supervise Tazzie's duties too.

Cathay watched Laura lean toward Elizabeth and whisper something in her ear. Elizabeth's face brightened and she stepped forward.

"I'll give you a cook," she said, "but you may not have Martha. You may have her girl here who works with her. She's young and strong and can cook anything you want."

Jim Long scowled and started to say no to her offer, but the colonel moved forward and answered before Long could continue.

"Fair enough. Get her ready. We'll take those provisions and things you've collected now. Then we'll leave first thing in the morning."

Cathay couldn't believe what she was hearing. She saw her mama's shoulders slump as Tazzie wrapped her arms around them in comfort.. Martha breathed heavily as she blinked back tears. Her eyes pleaded with Elizabeth who turned away and walked back into the house. Martha shook off Tazzie and followed.

Once inside Martha ran to Elizabeth.

"You can't mean that, Miz Elizabeth. Cathay don't know how to cook for no soldiers. She can't hardly boil water."

Elizabeth shrugged as she strolled arm in arm with her sister into the parlor.

Cathay couldn't move. She felt numb. She couldn't even think. The very thing her mama had dreaded for so long was finally happening. Only Cathay wasn't going to be sent to the fields. And she wasn't going to be sold. She was being given to the Union army. What would become of her when the soldiers found out she couldn't cook?

CHAPTER 7

The sun beamed down from high in the sky as young Cathay stood at the door of the smokehouse, a bundle containing all her possessions thrown over her shoulder. In one hand she clasped a sack containing a few biscuits and a slab of fatback her mama stuffed into it for her to take with her. Cathay knew Mama was not much at showing outward affection. All her love was stuffed with the food in that sack.

Martha stood at one side with her hands folded under her apron. Her head bowed as if in prayer.

Cathay reached into her apron pocket and fingered the tin soldier nestled there. No one knew of the bit of home she was taking away with her, and she thought of her desire to become like the military figures in Master Joseph's room. She had no idea then that her fantasy might come true, but not the way she intended.

The small band of slaves gathered in the quad between the smokehouse and the small garden behind the Johnson's plantation house. Cathay glanced beyond the garden to the knotted pecan tree where she retreated whenever she needed a place to dream. She'd discovered it years ago while hiding from Jasper and Henry, as they hunted for her to join them back at the quarters. It hid her well. Cathay's skin had blended with the dark brown, gnarled wood. The bushy limbs had camouflaged her twisted braids as she nestled among the leaves.

A bit of yearning gripped her. She realized the tree would no longer shelter her nor provide her with comfort.

Cathay pressed her side and felt the sharpness of the tin soldier in her pocket. Her souvenir would remind her of the battlefields she wanted to be a part of. Her throat tightened. She thought of how she often worried when some of the field hands she knew were sold. But her master had always chosen to keep his house servants. Martha, his main cook, had been allowed to stay. She had been certain Cathay would be too.

Yet, now Cathay was being sent away with Union soldiers.

Tears slid down Cathay's face as she looked up at her mama. Martha took a deep breath and tried to console herself and Cathay.

"There's no future here for you, gal," she said. She knew Cathay was being forced to go with the field slaves. "You can make yourself useful just like you been doing here with me. Just remember to keep your own counsel."

Cathay regretted not watching her mama more closely when Martha had tried to show her how to cook. Cathay's mind had always been cluttered with dreams of being free and going up north to find her father. She'd heard he was a freed man who passed through the area and then moved on up north.

Her mama had shushed her whenever she attempted to ask about her father. Few of the children Cathay's age knew who their real parents were, and Martha knew it was dangerous to talk about any of them that were freed. Cathay had been lucky that her mama had so far been able to keep her and her cousin, Jasper. At least Jasper would be going along with her when they left with the soldiers.

Martha raised her hand from under her apron and pushed Cathay toward the group that moved up the path alongside the house. Colonel Benton waited as his band of soldiers loaded Cathay, Jasper, Henry, and the other slaves and their meager belongings into wagons; wagons that would take them to who knows where?

The field hands didn't speak. No one wept. They were used to the mean treatment by Long, the overseer; change came to them often. The next time in their lives couldn't be much worse than times before. Their faces were set hard as statues as the wagons rolled down the road away from the plantation. Only Cathay turned a tear-streaked face to take one last look at her mama, the only home she'd ever known, and the place she hoped she would someday see again.

PART TWO
TRAVEL WITH THE UNION ARMY
LATE 1861-1866

CHAPTER 8

The wagons rattled through the Missouri countryside toward Arkansas. Cathay watched the familiar green and golden prairie change into dark walnut woods, and finally into the fog-shrouded Ozark Mountains. The sight of the blue-hazed peaks made her tremble with apprehension as they traveled day after day.

Cathay had seen fog before, but never trees and hills so completely concealed. As they moved along, it seemed as if each step would plunge them into nothingness. She dreaded the nights even more. The darkness and fog mingled, wrapped around them, and obscured everything and everyone only several feet away.

Since the soldiers used the wagons for more supplies gathered from the farms and towns they passed, the weary slaves were forced to walk. The only bed Cathay could claim was the cold Missouri ground. She used her bundle of clothes for a pillow, but only slept a little under her sackcloth shawl. She imagined animals roaming down from the mountains. The illusions kept her awake. When she did doze, Cathay dreamed. Ghosts, images of slaves who had been sold, hovered over her. She would wake hearing sobs ringing in her head, only to realize they were her own lonely cries for her home and mama far away.

Soldiers drafted more slaves from farms along the march. They came with tales of freedom that spread through the group.

"We gonna be free," Jasper said to Cathay one day. He'd heard the talk from some of the newcomers. "I heard they gonna let us go soon."

"And then where we goin'?" asked Cathay.

"Maybe up north," replied Henry, repeating the gossip. But he had no more idea of their destination than she.

Cathay didn't feel free. Regiment guards watched them closely because they were considered contraband, goods taken during a war. Since their masters had owned them, she knew the army considered them to be property that could be taken just as anything else they captured. One owner just changed to another. Cathay and the other slaves had no compass. Nor could they read a road map if they had one. There was nothing they could do but go along with the soldiers. The promise of freedom kept them from trying to escape. They would just wait.

Martha had told Cathay to "keep your own counsel." Cathay knew her mama meant that she should only depend on herself for survival. So Cathay watched and listened as the soldiers went about their duties around the camp.

Cooking over a campfire presented a challenge for Cathay. She didn't know how to make a fire or fix the salt pork or the cabbages and beans her mistress gathered for the soldiers. Nor did she know what to do with other foods such as eggs, corn, and fish collected from farms, fields, and streams as they passed. All she'd ever had to do was stir whatever her mama placed in a kettle and make sure it didn't burn or boil over.

She tried to hide among the few other women who came from some of the farms and relied on them to do whatever cooking the soldiers needed. She hoped the colonel would forget she was supposed to cook once the troops settled at a fort.

"Do you know how to cook?" she once asked Susie, a field hand about her age.

"I can cook grits and fatback," said Susie, "but that's all. My mama always cooked greens and stuff from the garden. Why you askin'?"

"I figured you 'n me could stick together when we gets to camp. I don't know how to cook neither."

"Lord, you a house gal and can't cook?" exclaimed Susie. "What you been doin'?"

Cathay threw her shoulders back, lifted her chin and answered with her eyes flashing in anger. "I can do laundry and make beds and do mending."

Susie just shook her head in amazement.

* * *

All along the march, Cathay heard loud booms in the distance. At first she thought they were sounds of thunder, but there was no rain. Also, the sounds didn't rumble like they did when a storm came; the rumbles like her mama called sounds of drums of the ancient ones that came from across the water. The sounds Cathay heard were sudden and explosive.

Boom! Pause. *Boom!*

After the explosions, soldiers came and ordered a few men to bring pitchforks and shovels and follow them. Once, Henry was in the group. When he returned, his face was ashen.

"What ails you?" Cathay whispered. "Where you been? You look like you seen the devil hisself."

Henry dropped his knees to the ground and put his head in his hands. When he looked up his eyes were red and filled with tears.

"The soldiers was fightin'. Bodies strewed all over the ground. We could smell the gunpowder in the air. We had to take our pitchforks and dig graves and bury them dead bodies." Henry looked like he was about to vomit.

Cathay never asked about any of the missions again.

CHAPTER 9

The trek was long and hard. Blisters appeared on the bottom of Cathay's feet as stones pierced through the thin soles of her shoes. The soldiers used up all the food provisions they had collected from the farms along the route. The food Martha had prepared for Cathay lasted only a few days. Afterward, the slaves received leftovers from the soldiers' meals. Hardtack, the mixture of flour, water, lard, and salt, was all they could expect. Occasionally they might get a piece of salt pork.

One day, some of the soldiers spotted fish as they marched alongside a stream. Cathay, standing nearby, heard one of the soldiers call some of the older slaves.

"You boys know how to catch these fish?" they asked.

"Yassuh," said one of them.

"Catch some then. We can use some more provisions."

Cathay watched as a slave tore strips of cloth from his shirt to make fishing lines, while others dug for beetles and night crawlers for bait. The men tied the lines to sticks and twigs and baited them. Some of the slaves removed their shirts to use as nets. Cathay knew these were some of the foraging skills their African ancestors had handed down from father to son. Those fishing skills often kept slaves from being hungry when meals were scarce on the plantation.

Soon the men returned with a few fish and gave them to the soldiers.

"These are great," the soldiers said as they took the fish away to be cooked.

But the slaves weren't allowed to eat any of them.

* * *

As the troops and their group of slaves reached Fort Rolla, Missouri, on the way to Little Rock, the only food left was hardtack and fat back. All of it was moldy. Years of poor nourishment and lack of comforts hardened most of the slaves. But even the lowliest slave managed better on the march than many of the Union soldiers. Some came from homes of privilege and wealth. While the slaves were used to surviving on meager rations and hard physical labor, the men in the Union army were often students or clerks or sons of shopkeepers and merchants. The long journey, frequent small battles, and poor food wore most of them down. Many became ill and some even died from malnutrition.

Since Cathay had been a house servant, and she and Jasper often got leftover food from the Johnson's kitchen, they were healthier than some of the others. But as they arrived at Fort Rolla, their stomach's groaned in empty rebellion.

At Fort Rolla, the soldiers rested. The slaves could not. They had to continue working; mending harnesses and clothing, serving meals, taking care of livestock and doing any other chores that needed to be done. Cathay wished she could be with Jasper. Since he had worked in the stables at the Johnson's farm, he worked caring for the officers' horses. He found he was busier than ever.

Colonel Benton called the food detail sergeant and pointed out Cathay. "I brought you another cook to help Ephraim in the kitchen. Hustle her along and get her started," he said, and walked away toward the camp office.

Cathay started to cry and wring her hands. "Sergeant, I can't cook," she protested. "I can just do some things..., uh like...uh...uh...washin' clothes... an...uh... an'...uh...cleanin'..., stuff like that."

"You'd better learn," growled the sergeant. "The colonel said you were to cook with Ephraim. You'll learn or by golly he'll tan your hide."

Cathay knew what that meant. That meant a whipping. Often her mama had threatened to "tan her hide" if she didn't mind. While Martha never did, Cathay had seen some of the other children whipped. She remembered Jasper's whipping the time he sassed Jim Long; the long streaks of bloodied flesh across his back; the thickened scars that remained long after the wounds healed. She had also seen field hands beaten with a whip by the overseer when they slacked off working.

Oh, Lord, what's gonna become-a me now.

The sergeant took Cathay to the post kitchen and introduced her to Ephraim, the cook, a huge, muscular, mahogany-colored man. Whenever he spoke and gave orders, his voice roared. Cathay trembled whenever she heard him.

She also met Lubelle, the tiny servant who looked like a little gingerbread doll. She had a complexion the color of slightly creamed coffee and always served the soldiers in the mess tent with a ready grin. With a colorful bandanna wrapped expertly around her head, Lubelle was as kindly as Ephraim was gruff. A bit over four feet, Lubelle kept up a steady stream of friendly, constant chatter. Her tiny frame also belied her strength. She hoisted loaded tray after loaded tray of meals from the kitchen to the mess hall without a stumble or complaint. The soldiers liked Lubelle and often passed her a coin as she slipped them an extra piece of cornbread or a sweetmeat. She reminded Cathay of Tazzie, the cheerful upstairs maid at the Johnson's plantation. Lubelle stood so tiny as Cathay's five feet nine inches towered above her, it made Cathay feel gawky and even less competent.

Ephraim was not tolerant when Cathay made mistakes with the cooking or the serving. More than once she dropped trays of food she carried, and often spilled liquid as she tried to serve the soldiers. Often she ran to Lubelle for refuge.

"Don't you worry about that big old blow mouth, Chile," Lubelle would say as she'd try to console Cathay when she made mistakes. "Lubelle help you learn your work."

But Cathay continued to struggle in the kitchen. She watched as the male slaves that escaped from some of the plantations earned their freedom by joining the Union soldiers. She wished she could just go work with the soldiers too. Their parading and practicing military maneuvers seemed far more interesting than working with Ephraim and Lubelle.

One time, Cathay was left in charge of making grits for breakfast. She tried to remember how Mama cooked them. Cathay placed the round black cook pot too close to the fire. When the water boiled, she poured the white cereal grains into the kettle. They foamed up and careened over the sides like an erupting volcano. Cathay jumped up and down waving a towel trying to fan the bubbling froth back into the pot. Lubelle came running, removed the pot, and threw cold salt water on the foam.

"Lawd, Chile, you better get yourself a mop and clean up this mess before Ephraim tans your hide."

Lubelle took the pot away and finished making the grits.

Even though Cathay learned some cooking little by little, Ephraim complained about how worthless she was as a cook's helper. He complained so much that the post sergeant finally assigned Cathay to do the laundry for the officers instead.

Her job as a laundress was not easy. She had to fill the heavy tubs with water and scrub the uniforms, socks and underwear on a board by hand. Cathay had to make sure she always had enough necessary items such as soap, starch for the shirts, and polish for the brass buttons. It was her job to carry the heavy 25 gallon laundry tubs whenever the soldiers were on the march. Her size, strength, and determination helped her to do the best she could at whatever task she was given. Relieved of her cooking duties, Cathay began to take pride in her job as one of the laundresses.

CHAPTER 10

One day Lubelle ran to where Cathay was sorting the officer's uniforms. Lubelle's customarily neat bandanna hung twisted and tilted over one eye. Her usual happy face frowned as if she had a pain.

"What's wrong, Lu?" asked Cathay.

Lubelle hiccupped as she tried to tell Cathay about Ephraim.

"When I was out back snappin' beans, I heard a ruckus in the mess tent. That big old clumsy Sergeant Graves was yelling at Ephraim. Seems the sergeant broke his tooth on something and blamed it on Ephraim's cooking."

Lubelle spoke without taking a breath. She shuddered slightly before continuing.

"Ephraim told the sergeant his teeth were just rotten, and it had nothin' to do with the way he fixed the food. Sergeant Graves grabbed Ephraim and hauled him outside. I don't know where he's takin' him, but I knows we got to do somethin' about dinner."

Cathay pushed the uniforms to one side and followed Lubelle to the mess tent where Lubelle finished cooking dinner with Cathay's help. When the meal was ready, Lubelle dished up the food while Cathay served the soldiers.

Later, Sergeant Graves came back and told Lubelle that Ephraim had been taken to the stockade.

"You're gonna do the cooking," he said, "and Cathay'll have to help."

Once again, Cathay was assigned to the kitchen. Only now she had to do laundry *and* kitchen duty.

Some of the slaves told Cathay that Ephraim looked as though he had been beaten. They said his eyes were swollen and his face, puffy and scratched. Later, he'd escaped and struck out through the woods. While the soldiers hunted for him, they didn't say they caught him.

Even though she never liked Ephraim much, Cathay still hoped he'd made it to freedom. She knew he would be alright if he could hook up with another Union regiment. But they were still in Confederate territory and there was a good chance Ephraim might get caught by Confederate troops, slave peddlers, or even some local slave owners. If that happened, he would be beaten and taken back to someplace as a slave again.

* * *

Soon Colonel Benton's troops were on the move again and Cathay along with them. But Lubelle stayed at Fort Rolla. That meant Cathay had to do laundry *and* cooking on the march. But she remembered Lubelle's tips about cooking.

Working with Lubelle had been far easier than working with Ephraim. What she learned from Lubelle helped her manage the meals and cooking better than when she first arrived at the fort. She had watched Lubelle more closely than she had watched her mama. She'd had a feeling cooking might have to be her job again. And it was.

Eventually, Colonel Benton left the army to return to his home in Indiana. Cathay watched as the colonel's horse and his escort rode away. She felt betrayed by the colonel's leaving. He could go back to his home. She could never go back to hers. Just when she was beginning to feel secure in Colonel Benton's Union Army regiment, she would be forced to adjust to a new commander.

General Samuel Ryan Curtis took over the command, and the 13th Missouri regiment became part of the 8th Indiana Hoosiers. That meant Cathay had to go wherever the Hoosiers went. She would have to live the rugged life in camp tents, while the Union soldiers chased the Confederate army toward northwest Arkansas.

Meanwhile, Cathay's cooking skills improved more and more. She began to experiment with changing some of the dishes she learned from Lubelle. Her specialty was a fish stew made with onions and okra and some of the herbs and spices Lubelle showed her.

The new commander, General Curtis, summoned the mess sergeant.

"Who made this stew?" he asked.

"Sorry, sir," the sergeant apologized. He thought the general was displeased. "I won't let that gal do any more cooking".

"Not do any more cooking!" roared the general. "I want *more* of her cooking. This is the best tasting food I've had since I took over this command." He ordered the mess sergeant to give Cathay fewer laundry jobs so she could devote more time to cooking.

The 8th Indiana finally became a part of the Army of the Southwest. As they moved toward Arkansas, Cathay became their number one cook.

CHAPTER 11

Fighting became more and more intense. The tenacious General Curtis pushed the troops further toward the Arkansas border. Intent on winning Missouri for the Union, he led the soldiers through rigorous campaigns, over the rough mountainous terrain of the Ozark Mountains, just north of Arkansas. Cathay found breathing difficult and her work more tiring in the thin air of the higher elevations. Her legs and feet ached as she marched alongside the troops in frosty temperatures up and down hills and across icy streams.

General Curtis complained about the lack of supplies, especially clothing and shoes for the soldiers. Still they were better than those of Cathay and the other slaves, many who wore some of the same clothes they brought from the plantation. Cathay had made a shawl out of a blanket that one of the soldiers discarded and it served to keep her comfortable during the cold higher regions. Mama had said, *Keep your own counsel,* and Cathay remembered and survived.

Thunderous booms of cannon fire could be heard as they moved into the area called Pea Ridge, a mountainous section of Arkansas covered with forest and the wild peas that gave it its name. The soldiers encountered more battles and there were more injuries. Cathay and the laundresses had the added job of nursing the wounded. Cathay remembered how back on the plantation, the older women doctored sick slaves with healing herbs their African mothers taught them how to gather. Few masters would call a doctor for an ailing servant.

Just like them women back on the plantation, she thought. *I is learning nursing. Something else 'sides cooking and laundering.*

* * *

One day, when a new group of injured soldiers arrived in camp, Cathay saw her cousin, Jasper, one of the stretcher bearers.

Cathay hadn't seen Jasper since they left Fort Rolla, but she knew he was still with the regiment. Some of the laundresses and other workers had seen him caring for the horses along the march. Cathay ran to him. The bearers set the stretcher down and Jasper hugged her.

"Hey there, Cathay. Good to see you."

Jasper was leaner and taller than she remembered, but he did not look tired or sick. Also a slight fuzz covered his upper lip and chin.

"You look like you got yourself a beard and mustache," Cathay teased. "I expect you think you's all growed up."

Jasper frowned, shook his head, and ignored her teasing.

He pointed to the soldier on the stretcher. "I brought some work for you, but I can't stay. They's lots a hurt men out there. I be bringing more and more directly. Gotta go."

As Jasper hurried off, Cathay sighed. Her cousin had lost his lighthearted air; she noticed his somber and unsmiling manner. Seeing Jasper reminded her how much she missed him and her mama back on the plantation.

* * *

As Cathay pulled down the covering from the soldier Jasper had just brought in, she saw an opening in his shoulder. Dirt covered the wound. She washed the soldier's chest and carefully cleaned the flesh around the hole. She placed a clean piece of a sheet over it until the camp surgeon could remove the bullet or the pieces of shell. The soldier groaned in pain.

"You gonna be just fine," Cathay crooned. "Doctor's gonna fix you up and you be better'n ever."

As she sponged the soldier's face, hoping to give him some comfort, Cathay's hands ached from the cold. When she tried to give another soldier a drink of water, she could hardly handle the mug. She rubbed her hands together briskly to warm them. She raised the soldier's head, and guided the cup to his lips. Then, gently she lowered the his head, and moved on to another.

The Pea Ridge Battle forced Cathay to confront war and all its horrors. It was Cathay's first experience with the cruel effects of war. Wounded soldiers were everywhere. The smell of blood reminded her of William Johnson's sick room. Only now she had no mama to shield her from the odors surrounding the sick. At times she'd have to leave the infirmary tent so no one would see her gag.

After the Pea Ridge battle, General Curtis and the Army of the Southwest continued through the Ozarks and onward through Arkansas.

Cathay still wore the thin, buttoned, castoff shoes that William Johnson gave his slaves. By now they were worn to shreds, but her blisters had healed and the long hours standing as a laundress and cook had formed calluses on her feet. The soldiers' boots of sturdier leather were frayed also, but able to better withstand long marches. Cathay hoped the army would give her heavier footwear when they reached the next fort.

Often wrecked supply lines meant there was very little food. Cathay recalled her trek from the Johnson Plantation to Fort Rolla. That wasn't easy either. She had managed then and would survive the present hardships as well. As she suffered hunger in the cold weather with the soldiers, she began to feel like a part of the army. She still kept the kneeling soldier with her belongings and that gave her comfort. While Cathay knew of no women soldiers in the army, she still thought it would be an exciting life to lead. She'd always enjoyed playing with the boys on the plantation although Mama disliked her rough-housing. She imagined herself being free and wearing the striking blue uniform of the Union warriors she marched alongside.

General Curtis' Army of the Southwest advanced across Missouri, across northern Arkansas and southeast along the Mississippi River to Helena, Arkansas. Cathay showed she had the stamina to match many of the soldiers, and the heart to survive all the obstacles she faced.

As they arrived at Camp Helena, Cathay encountered many freed and runaway slaves who saw the presence of the Union Army as refuge from the Confederacy and their slave masters. Although she was still a servant of the army and had not been freed by it, the presence of freedmen around her seemed to mean a promise of liberation from the hated plantation drudgery.

The slaves were all quartered in a squalid contraband camp. Packed in close quarters, they often had to sleep in tents on mats or the ground. Men and women suffered from dysentery and cholera brought on by poor food and unhealthy drinking water from the Mississippi River. Cathay developed a fever and constant headaches, but still she went about her daily chores. No longer needed as a nurse, she still worked in the mess hall and in the laundry areas.

Throughout the day, Cathay went about her chores in a trance as though she were somebody else. Day after day she dragged her exhausted, aching body from her camp quarters to the mess hall to the laundry tub. At night she slept as though she were dead. Gradually, Cathay's strength and determination helped her to recover. Other weaker members in the camp did not.

Although work at Camp Helena was hard, Cathay soon became used to the routine. She actually began to enjoy her mess hall assignments as more and more of the soldiers commented on how much they enjoyed her cooking. Of course her biggest compliments came from General Curtis.

Just as she settled into the satisfaction of being in a permanent camp, Cathay received an unexpected order.

CHAPTER 12

One day, the mess sergeant came to Cathay with a new command.

"You're going to be sent to Little Rock," he said. "General Curtis wants you to do more cooking and you can learn more at the camp there."

"I knows enough to satisfy most-a these folks here," Cathay protested. "Especially General Curtis."

The sergeant grunted. "You just get your stuff together and be ready to travel." He put his hands on his hips, thrust his chin forward, and growled. "You go wherever you're sent."

Cathay shuffled off to pack her few belongings. She didn't want to go away from the people she had become to know and things she had learned. Cathay wasn't ready to move to another place.

But she had no choice. She was still a slave and those were her orders. She had to obey them. Cathay wished she could find Jasper to say goodbye. The camp was spread out but she knew her cousin worked with the horses. He often slept with the cavalry and rarely came to the contraband quarters. She couldn't leave a note because Cathay had never learned to read or write. The best she could do was send him word by one of the young boys that carried messages back and forth throughout the camp.

After packing her sack, Cathay trudged up the road to see if she could find a messenger. She passed the Helena stockade and guardhouse with its narrow grilled windows. She glanced at the bakery that sat just behind the mess hall kitchen where she had spent long hours over hot fires, preparing meals for several hundred or so Union soldiers, officers and camp workers. Near the camp office, she spotted her friend, Henry, who was one of the messengers.

"Will you tell Jasper I'm being sent to Little Rock to learn cooking? He probably working with the cavalry horses. I hope I sees him somewhere some other time. I hope I sees you again too."

As Cathay stood with the other cooks being sent to Little Rock, she thought about how families on the plantation were broken up and sent away, never to see each other again. Being sent to Little Rock wasn't much different. As she waited for the wagon to take the cooks, she spotted a group of colored soldiers on horseback nearby. They wore the blue uniforms of the Union Army, but were not as striking as the white soldiers. Their uniforms were dusty and somewhat threadbare. Still she trembled with excitement to see them; to see people with her skin color, free to be a part of the Union Army. Although not free, she felt safe when she found out she and the other cooks were going to go to Little Rock in the company of these men.

Once again, Cathay was departing for a new destination. This time she was not as fearful as she had once been. Although she felt a little nervous as she climbed into the wagons with her companions, Cathay was determined more than ever to be the best at whatever anyone assigned her to do. She would conquer her fears at Little Rock as she had at Fort Rolla, Pea Ridge, and the Helena camp.

CHAPTER 13

Once Cathay arrived at the encampment outside Little Rock, her duties were mostly cooking. Since the Union Army under Generals Herron and Blunt had recently defeated the Confederate Army, Cathay enjoyed more freedom working in the mess hall than she ever had at Fort Rolla or Camp Helena. She and the other cooks learned a lot; much more than she had imagined. Mostly, they learned how to cook on the march using supplies they found along the way. Fish was often plentiful. Farms and plantations still provided potatoes and corn and many times they came across an abandoned garden or fruit tree. She thought. *Mama would sure be proud-a how far I got.*

When the new regiment began moving, Cathay and other servants traveled with ex-slaves and colored Union soldiers, since the freed slaves and colored soldiers were kept apart from the white military. She had improved so much at Little Rock that she became the main cook. She made decisions about what all of the soldiers ate, and rarely did anyone object. At Little Rock, she had learned to cook and bake on the trail. The lessons had served her well. Sweet potatoes and fish stew were her favorites, and the white soldiers loved her food as much as General Curtis. *I'm just like Ephraim,* she thought. *And a little like Mama.* The thought made a smile flicker across her face.

As the Army of the Southwest moved its campaign through Georgia, Alabama, and Mississippi, Cathay saw the gruesome results the war left. Everywhere the regiment went there were fire-blackened fields, once white with cotton. Cathay saw the mansions on southern plantations, now mere skeletons of their former stately selves. She remembered Miz Elizabeth and her sister, Miz Laura, and what Jonah told her of how their house and fields had been burned. He said they had barely escaped with their lives. She wondered if that was like what she was seeing. *Did the Union soldiers burn these fields and houses? What about the Johnson Plantation? Did Mama and the others she left behind survive?*

One night, when the regiment was camped near a Louisiana harbor, Cathay was awakened by a strange roar. It sounded like a soft explosion, a *whoof* off in the distance. Cathay left her pallet and crept to the door of the servants' tent. The night glowed red and flames shot high into the sky.

"What's all that red over there?" she asked another slave who watched with her.

"I think they's burning boats in the water," came the reply. "The Union Army sets fire to gunboats filled with cotton that's moored in the harbor. The rebs use the boats to send bales of cotton they call "white gold" up the Red River and across the Rio Grande to Mexico. They sell the cotton to buy arms and supplies to use against the Union Army."

Cathay smelled the scorched air as sparks flitted like fireflies across the water. *Wonder how many peoples was on them boats,* Cathay thought. The sight of the burning ships made Cathay shiver.

That part of the war chilled Cathay, and she shook her head at the thought of it.

Still, Cathay found camp life fascinating. Hundreds of slave workers traipsed behind the army, plantation workers liberated by the Union Army. There was always something happening in the hub-bub of camp activity; drills; regiments coming and going; wounded arriving from the battlefield; and her own duties as cook and sometimes laundress or nurse. Traveling with the army from place to place gave her an inside look at the life of a soldier.

From time to time Cathay would pull out the tin soldier she took from Master Joseph's room, finger it, and pretend *she* was that kneeling soldier.

CHAPTER 14

Cathay stood with the other servants on the dock in the Mississippi Valley. She eyed the steamboat in front of her with some apprehension.

"Wonder why we gots to go on this big boat?" Cathay asked no one in particular.

Several of the other servants standing nearby heard her question. One of them answered. "Maybe they wants us to get up the road quicker'n we can go by walking." He chuckled.

The soldiers pushed the slaves toward the gangplank and they boarded. Cathay looked down from the deck at the dark water of the Gulf of Mexico. The water looked cold and dangerous. It moved back and forth, slapping the side of the steamship. *Slap. Slap.* Cathay stumbled as she boarded, and her stomach lurched. A bitter, gall-like taste came into her mouth and she groaned. Afraid she was going to be sick; she took deep breaths and swallowed hard. She took another breath and grasped the ship's rail.

All of Cathay's travels had been on land. Sometimes she marched with the troops. Sometimes she rode with the other servants in wagons. The steamboat ride became another adventure she would have to endure. As the boat rocked from side to side, Cathay didn't know what to expect.

While she waited for the soldiers to tell her where to go on the boat, Cathay overheard Captain Gibbs, the steamboat captain, arguing with a woman on the dock. The woman was trying to board with four small children.

"Madam, I have no room for passengers," Cathay heard Captain Gibbs say. "We are transporting soldiers and their servants to Washington City and have no place where you can stay."

"Captain," protested the woman, "I have my daughter and three small sons with me. My husband is an officer in the Union Army and is waiting for us in Shenandoah. This is the last steamer leaving for the north. I will NOT expose my children to disease in this godforsaken city." Cathay watched the woman tip her chin up in defiance, her eyes flashing with anger.

Captain Gibbs blew out a deep breath in frustration and shrugged. He stared at the woman for a moment and then said softly, "I understand. I have one stateroom down in the hold next to the storeroom where the servants stay. It is dark and may be wet when the sailors swab the decks."

"We'll take it with our gratitude," said the woman. Cathay saw the woman hurry away to gather her children and belongings. Just then the Union Sergeant Dawes herded all the servants below to their crowded quarters. Cathy did not see the woman board.

In the storeroom the slaves sat on benches, hip to hip, with their bundles behind their legs or propped in front of their feet. There was no space to lie down and Cathay wondered if they were expected to sleep at all during the journey.

Once she became used to the boat's rocking, it soothed Cathay somewhat, and she remembered Miz Alice rocking her babies back on the plantation. *Maybe this trip won't be so bad after all. I slept under worse conditions before.*

A loud blast from the boat's horn caused Cathay to jump. It signaled the boat's departure. Cathay heard a banging disturbance outside the door of the storeroom. She wondered if the woman and her children were being placed in the stateroom the captain indicated. *Would she get a chance to see them? What were they like?*

A sudden bump shocked Cathay from her thoughts. The gentle rocking became a thrust that threatened to throw the slaves from their benches. No longer did Cathay think she was being rocked to sleep. Her apprehension returned and she braced herself for another new trial.

CHAPTER 15

On the open waters of the Atlantic Ocean, the steamboat tossed violently. Cathay's stomach churned and at times she retched with dry heaves. While some of the slaves sat stoically throughout the journey, others moaned and retched like Cathay. If any slept, it was done on another's shoulder or in someone's lap. They had nowhere to relieve themselves except in their clothes. Gradually the stench became almost as unbearable as the seasickness.

The sailors passed out gruel for the slaves to eat once a day, but they ate very little. Conditions erased any appetite they may have had. Cathay longed for the day she would again be allowed to cook for the soldiers. *Mama, what a change in me! Would you believe it? I actually wanna cook!* But the thought of food only made her stomach churn again.

* * *

Fifteen days later, the slaves left their stinking, stuffy quarters and climbed to the decks for their first breath of fresh air in Washington City. Cathay looked around for the woman and her children, but she did not see them. She hoped the woman's husband was able to greet them. Cathay wished she had someone like Jasper and his friend, Henry, to greet her. But there was only the sharp talking Sergeant Dawes to herd them as she and the other servants disembarked.

"Get over there so's we can load you up. You folks going to Virginia, so get a move on."

As they climbed into the wagons, Cathay gazed around at sights she had never seen before. A huge round dome, the dome of the U.S. Capital building, dominated the scene. Black and white people bustled through the streets where the wagon traveled toward the capital parade grounds. There, a smelly Cathay, alongside her stinking fellow-servants, emerged to join the soldiers of the 8th Indiana regiment they had been serving. Gathering their bundles of belongings, they began the trek to Berryville, Virginia, where they were finally able to clean themselves and begin their duties as before.

In Virginia, the 8th Indiana Hoosiers came under the command of another general, General William H. Emory. Cathay served the Hoosiers under four other commanders until she finally came to the attention of a feisty Irish general, Philip Sheridan. Since she had served the Indiana regiment as the chief cook and sometimes laundress, Cathay was assigned to General Sheridan and his staff.

Soon the 8th Indiana Hoosiers were reassigned to still another officer, General Frederick Steel. But General Sheridan made one exception.

"I'll keep that gal that's been cooking and serving me," he demanded as he took over the Army of the Shenandoah. "I don't want to have to get used to another servant who doesn't know the way I like things done."

Cathay liked General Sheriden. He reminded her of General Curtis. She felt content to travel with him on his campaigns. Often, though, she was somewhat lonely for the acquaintances and other servants of the Indiana Regiment. She missed those with whom she had traveled so long.

Sheridan's campaigns took him from Washington to Virginia and Iowa. Often Cathay found herself along with the Union Army, scrambling from Rebel Confederate Soldier attacks. She often told herself, *I knows I better get away if I don't want to be captured and have to spend the rest of my life on plantations again.* However, she became a part of the victories as well. Cathay observed the famous "Sheridan's Ride" when the general saved a major battle at Cedar Creek. She observed the Union Army's gradual successes as the Civil War eventually came to an end and Cathay returned to an area ten miles south of St. Louis, Missouri.

CHAPTER 16

Cathay Williams was free.

She had made a circuitous journey from slavery in Missouri, not far from where she had grown up, to freedom there as well.

"What do you plan to do now the war's over?" General Sheridan asked Cathay, as he dismissed his staff. "I'm not going to need freed slaves tagging along with me when I go south to my new post. You're going to be on your own."

Many of the freed slaves did not know what to do with themselves with no master to direct them. Most of the soldiers under General Sheridan's command did not like his brash way of talking and giving orders. He was not at all like Colonel Benson or even General Curtis. But Cathay was used to serving under all kinds of commanders and had earned the respect of all of them, even Phiipl Sheridan. She was surprised that he even asked what she was planning. She had learned to survive as a slave, and learned skills as a servant for the military. She knew she could make her own way somehow.

"I don't want to be a burden to nobody," Cathay answered. "I reckon I'll find somebody that wants me to cook or wash for them."

"I have a friend in St. Louis," said General Sheridan. "I can put in a good word for you, but you'll have to get there somehow on your own. I can't give you any transportation." He pulled out a piece of paper and wrote a note along with the name of Julia Powers, 160 Front Street, St. Louis, Missouri.

"I thank you, sir. I knows I can get there." Cathay took the paper, and when she had gathered her few belongings, she left the General's command office.

PART THREE
BUFFALO SOLDIERS
1866-1868

CHAPTER 17

"Can you point me the way to St. Louis?" Cathay asked one of the men outside General Sheridan's office. After adjusting her pack of belongings to a more comfortable place on her back, she struck out in the direction he pointed. Most of Cathay's travel with the Union Army had been on foot, except those times when the soldiers piled the slaves in wagons to transport them to another camp. As horses and wagons and carriages passed her, no one stopped to offer her a ride. Nor did she even consider riding.

Lost in her own thoughts, Cathay wondered if her mama knew she was free. Had Miz Elizabeth sent Mama away or kept her on the plantation? Cathay knew Mama was a great cook and could get a job anywhere, but she hoped Miz Elizabeth would let Mama stay on after the war as a paid servant.

A rumbling in her stomach reminded Cathy that she had not eaten anything before she left General Sheridan. Most of the road to St. Louis ran alongside fields of hemp and tobacco, much like the crop on the Johnson Plantation. However, as she strolled along, she spied a field that looked like it contained sugarcane. Remembering how she and Jasper used to chew on cane stalks when they were children, Cathay looked around to be sure no one was looking. She walked over to the field and broke off a piece of one of the plants. Then she returned to the road. Chewing on the cane stalk helped to ease her hunger.

Several hours later, Cathay approached the city of St. Louis. Since she did not know how to find the person General Sheridan had written on the note she carried, Cathay had to find someone to direct her to the address of the general's friend. She spied an old man walking with a cane along one of the streets leading into the city. She showed him General Sheridan's note, but the old man shook his head and pointed to a group of young people who were gathered around a fountain in the town square. Cathay hurried to them and showed them the note.

Soon she found herself standing at the back door of a modest house on Front Street where one of the young people had directed her. A tall, thin colored woman, wearing a gray maid's uniform and lacy white apron, answered her knock and took the note Cathay handed her.

While she waited at the door, Cathay looked around her. The well cared for grounds contained a neatly trimmed hedge row between the Powers' house and the neighbor, only a stone's throw away. A wide expanse of lawn and several beds of colorful flowers adorned the back yard, but all along the street, the houses were similarly close to their neighbors. Cathay remembered the plantation house where she grew up. It sat far away from any other dwelling with only the washhouse and the smokehouse nearby. Even the stables lay further down the road from the big house, although the slave cabins down by the fields sat next to each other. She wondered if city people were friendly living so close.

A stout, jolly looking woman came to the door with the maid to whom Cathay had given the note.

"I'm Mrs. Powers," said the woman. "General Sheridan says you're a good laundress and a good cook. I don't need a cook, but I can use a good laundress and a maid for my daughter, Clara. I can pay you three dollars a month and give you room and board if you want the job." The woman had a kindly face but did not smile.

Cathay nodded and replied. "Yes'm, I do want the job. Thank you, ma'am."

"Daisy here will show you to your room and let you know what your chores will be," said Mrs. Powers, and returned back inside.

As she followed a straight-backed, unsmiling Daisy, Cathay looked around at the modest rooms of the Powers' home, not nearly as grand as those in the Johnson Plantation house. The maid led her up a carpeted stairway, past a landing where several doorways opened into bedrooms. They came to a narrow staircase and climbed to a garret floor that contained two small rooms. The ceilings were low and the floorboards squeaked as they walked across them.

"This here's my room," said Daisy as she pointed to the first room. A curtain, hanging from a rope across the top of the opening, served as a door. "You'll have to get your own curtain if you want one for your room," she said curtly. She pointed to the second open room. It had one small, high window with closed shutters. The room was bare except for a cot and a table next to it. There was no dresser or cabinet for her clothes. But the Cathay that had trekked through the roads and hills during the wars was glad she had a place to stay. She had her own room, and would get pay for the work she did.

Daisy retreated downstairs, leaving Cathay to herself, to reflect on her new job and her future. She stood and opened the window that overlooked other houses in the area.

Here I is, starting to do the same things Tazzie did at Master's house. Maybe I can get some work cooking later on. But at least it'll do for the time being. Cathay sat down on the cot for a few moments, breathed a deep sigh, and then found her way downstairs to see what her mistress expected her duties to be.

* * *

Every day she washed or ironed. She helped fifteen-year-old Clara Powers dress, and watched as she primped. Cathay listened as the pampered girl gave orders about everything from what she wanted to eat to what to wear and how she wanted her hair arranged. She found herself doing all of the hated and boring house chores she'd despised as a slave, and seized every chance she could to escape by running errands downtown.

CHAPTER 18

One day, on one of her trips into town, Cathay spotted her cousin, Jasper, sitting across from the rear steps of the St. Louis courthouse. Cathay hadn't seen Jasper since they'd been separated at Helena when she was sent to Little Rock to learn cooking. Jasper's arms were muscular and he looked healthy. He had a real mustache which gave him a manly appearance that he didn't have the last time she saw him.

Cathay ran across the road and called to him. "Hey there, Jasper." Jasper looked up at her and gave a broad grin. Cathay's smile gleamed back. She noticed Henry was with him. Henry always managed to stay with Jasper wherever he went. Not as brawny as Jasper, he also looked older and somewhat haggard.

"What y'all been doing since you left the army?" Cathay asked.

Jasper pointed to the wagon and the horses standing nearby.

"We been knocking around doing odd jobs here 'n there. I been helping out at the livery stable since I knows about horses. Henry can't find nothing but cleaning up 'cause he only worked the fields at Mastah Johnson's place. Nobody wants field hands here about now. But the man over at the livery stable said Henry could clean up around there."

Henry added. "We thinking about joining up with the army. They's gonna be just us colored soldiers. We knows soldiering and they say they gonna pay us. Pay be thirteen dollars a month. Jasper and me can still be together."

Henry tried to smile, and Cathay could see he had some missing teeth. Also, he seemed unsure about the soldiering idea. His shoulders drooped, and every now and then, his eye twitched. Cathay remembered how he had reacted when he had to bury dead soldiers, and wondered how he would make it in the army.

"I sure wish I could join up," said Cathay. "Sure would beat primping Miz Clara and washing her drawers every day. Miz Powers' daughter's a pain, she so prissy. Her mama spoils her and want her be just so."

Cathay kicked a stone and scuffed her heels in the dirt.

"Yeah," said Jasper. "I remember you went to Little Rock to learn to cook for soldiers in the Army."

"I been treatin' wounded men with General Sheriden too. I been in more battles than a lot of people. I ain't carried no gun, but I seen plenty shooting and done lots-a tramping."

Cathay's frame was tall, her build was stout, and she'd always been strong and muscular. For a few minutes, she and Jasper talked about their younger days.

"'Member how I used to wrastle with the boys on the plantation? I beat 'em most of the time. I bet I could still beat you'n Henry."

"I bet you can too," Henry said. He chuckled and gave her a snaggletooth grin.

"I can do better cooking for soldiers and won't have to do all that laundry," she continued. "I bet I can do soldiering just like you two."

They both sat for awhile, lost in their own thoughts; Cathay tracing circles in the dirt with her toe; Jasper quietly holding his head in his hands in thought. A few minutes later, he straightened up and said, "Why don't you get you some men's clothes and dress up like we do. Maybe you can join up too."

Henry slapped his leg and laughed out loud. Cathay was glad to see something perk him up.

"Won't that be something? Her soldiering and the army don't know nothing about her being a gal."

"Hush up," hissed Jasper. "Somebody might hear you." Then he turned to Cathay and spoke softly. "Go on. Do what you have to do. Won't nobody know but we two, and we won't blow on you."

Cathay looked down and continued to dig her toes in the dirt.

"Unh, unh. That might be something to think about." She slapped Jasper on the shoulder and started off to figure out how she would carry out such a plan.

CHAPTER 19

Cathay Williams stood outside the courthouse for a long time. She watched the line of colored men that formed in front of the enlistment table and her thoughts went back to the conversation she'd had with Jasper and Henry a few days earlier.

She'd told Miz Powers she had to go take care of her sick mama and didn't know when she could get back to work. Cathay didn't like lying to Miz Powers who trusted her. She was grateful that Miz Powers had been good enough to hire her when she was freed and left General

Sheridan. But Cathay couldn't tell Miz Powers about the idea of joining the army.

Cathay looked down at her baggy pants and shirt. No one seemed to notice any difference between her and the other would-be recruits. A soldier nearby seemed to think she was one of those waiting to enlist. That gave Cathay confidence as she moved into the enlistment line.

Tall and muscular with her short, wooly hair, she looked like the men in line. Also, she had lived with the army throughout the war and had begun to assume the walk, talk, and actions of a soldier.

Humph, Cathay thought. *I can do soldiering as well as any of these men here.* Since she had been at Cedar Creek and Pea Ridge and all over, from Washington to Virginia to Iowa, and back with General Sheridan, she thought she had observed everything about soldiering. Cathay had endured hunger and fatigue; battles and marches; tended the wounded and seen the dead buried.

Her thoughts were racing. *I knows all about fighting and about wounded and dying people, too.* But what did the army do now that the war was over? And what would she say when she reached the front of the line? What could she call herself? She'd fooled the soldier at the back of the enlistment line, but could she fool the recruiting officer?

And what would happen if the officer found out she was a woman?

Cathay began to think of easy names to go by. She thought of the Johnson Plantation and pondered over names she could call herself; names like Johnny Williams, or Willie Johnson.

She tried saying all different names to herself to hear what sounded right. Mama never told her the name of her daddy. It would have been nice to use his name. Whatever she called herself, it would have to be a name she could recognize easily if someone spoke to her.

Suddenly, she was standing in front of the recruitment desk.

"What's your name, boy?" the recruitment officer asked.

Cathay's mind went blank. She couldn't remember any of the names she had tried to use.

"Name's C-C-Cathay, sir," she stammered in a low voice.

The officer stared at her and waited. Cathay had to say something. She remembered her master's first name.

"Uh, William, sir."

"How old are you, William?"

"I think I'm 22."

Cathay tilted her head upward and threw her shoulders back.

"Well, William Cathay, are you sure you want to fight for the army of these United States?"

Cathay did not hesitate. "Yes, sir."

The officer wrote Cathay's new name on a paper and told her to read it and sign it.

"I ain't never knowed how to read, sir. Nobody never teached me."

The officer picked up the enlistment paper and read:

> *I, William Cathay, do solemnly swear,*
>
> *that I will bear true faith and allegiance to the United States of America,*
>
> *and that I will serve them honestly and faithfully against all their enemies.*

"Sign here," he said, and pointed to a line beneath the writing.

Cathay had no idea if the words on the paper were truly what the soldier read. She only knew that signing the paper would enlist her in the army. The officer had said her name backwards and that sounded alright. She had seen the other recruits write an X on the paper, so she took the pen the officer gave her and made a bold X mark in the space the officer indicated.

Cathay Williams had become William Cathay, a member of the United States Army.

DECLARATION OF RECRUIT.

I, *William Cathay* desiring
to ENLIST in the Army of the United States, for the term of THREE YEARS do declare, That I am
twenty one years and _____ months of age; that I have
neither wife nor child; that I have never been discharged from the United States service on account of
disability or by sentence of a court-martial, or by order before the expiration of the term of enlistment; and
I know of no impediment to my serving honestly and faithfully as a soldier for three years.

GIVEN at *Saint Louis Mo.*

The *15th* day of *November 1866*

William Cathay

Witness:

P.L. Sherman

No. *7535*

William Cathay

Enlisted at *St. Louis Mo.* on
the *15th* day of *November*, 18*66*,
by *Major H.C. Sherman*
38th Regiment of *Infantry*

Assigned to the *38th* Regiment of
Infantry U. S. Army.

_____ enlistment; last served in Company ( )

_____ Reg't of _____

Discharged _____, 18 .

DIRECTIONS.

Enlistments must, in all cases, be taken in triplicate. The recruiting
officer will send one copy to the Second Auditor with his monthly accounts,
a second to the superintendent with his monthly return, and a third to the
depot as the time the recruits are sent there. In case of soldiers re-enlisted
in a regiment, or of regimental recruits, the third copy of the enlistment
will be sent at its date to regimental headquarters for file.

Superintendents will endorse on the copy for the Adjutant General, the
regiment to which the recruit is assigned, in all enlistments made subsequent to December 31, 1865, before forwarding it in compliance with
paragraph 919, Revised Army Regulations; *provided* that the time required
to accomplish this shall not exceed four months, in which case it will be
forwarded without this information.

The names of all men enlisted during the month will appear upon the
Monthly Return, required by the paragraph above referred to; and of such
as are not assigned, a Muster and Descriptive Roll will be forwarded in
lieu of the copy of enlistment.

Enlistment papers, detained for assignment of the recruit, will be forwarded with subsequent Returns, with the names entered thereon in red
ink, but will not be enumerated with current enlistments as having been
enlisted during the month.

The death, desertion, or discharge of a recruit before assignment, will
be noted upon the enlistment, which will be forwarded to this Office with
the first subsequent Return.

CONSENT IN CASE OF MINOR.

STATE OF   TOWN OF

Missouri   *Saint Louis*

I, *William Cathey* born in *Independence* in the State of *Missouri*, aged *twenty-two* years, and by occupation a *Cook* Do HEREBY ACKNOWLEDGE to have voluntarily enlisted this *fifteenth* day of *November* 1866, as a **Soldier** in the Army of the United States of America, for the period of **THREE YEARS**, unless sooner discharged by proper authority: Do also agree to accept such bounty, pay, rations, and clothing, as are, or may be, established by law. And I, *William Cathey* do solemnly swear, that I will bear true faith and allegiance to the **United States of America**, and that I will serve them honestly and faithfully against all their enemies or opposers whomsoever; and that I will observe and obey the orders of the President of the United States, and the orders of the officers appointed over me, according to the Rules and Articles of War.

Sworn and subscribed to, at *St Louis Mo* this 15th day of *November* 1866. BEFORE *Henry Romeriam* *Major 38th Infty*

William   X   Cathey

I CERTIFY, ON HONOR, That I have carefully examined the above named recruit, agreeably to the General Regulations of the Army, and that in my opinion he is free from all bodily defects and mental infirmity, which would, in any way, disqualify him from performing the duties of a soldier.

C. M. Powers

Act. Asst. Surg U.S.A.
EXAMINING SURGEON.

I CERTIFY, ON HONOR, That I have minutely inspected the Recruit, *William Cathey* previously to his enlistment, and that he was entirely sober when enlisted; that, to the best of my judgment and belief, he is of lawful age; and that, in accepting him as duly qualified to perform the duties of an able-bodied soldier, I have strictly observed the Regulations which govern the recruiting service. This soldier has *black* eyes, *black* hair, *black* complexion, is *5* feet *9* inches high.

Henry Romeriam

Major 38 El I U.S.a.
RECRUITING OFFICER.

[A. G. O. No. 73.]

CHAPTER 20

Cathay Williams, now William Cathay, followed the other recruits to an area where they were directed by a sergeant in the blue uniform of the Union Army. The drab, dusty room had benches where the new recruits sat lined along three of the walls. Cathay wondered what would happen next. She didn't have long to wait.

"William Cathay!"

A voice boomed her name and startled her at first. It seemed strange to hear it; but at least she had no trouble recognizing her new name.

Cathay moved forward. The officer calling her name was the acting company doctor. He took her to a corner of the room and made her stand with her back against the wall facing the other recruits.

"Can you read this?" asked the doctor, holding up a card about ten feet in front of her.

"No, sir. I never learned to read, sir."

The doctor blew out a breath of exasperation.

"I mean can you see the letters."

"Yes, sir. I sees 'em."

He walked over and poked Cathay's arms and legs with his finger. "Open your mouth," he commanded.

Cathay did as she was told. The doctor rapped Cathay's teeth with a small metal hammer to see if her teeth were strong. The movement made her teeth tingle. He made her squeeze his hands to see how strong her hands were. They had to be strong enough to hold and shoot a rifle. He wrote something on a paper and pushed Cathay to join the other recruits. That was the end of the medical examination. The doctor called the next recruit.

Not realizing she had been holding her breath, Cathay exhaled a sigh of relief. The doctor hadn't noticed that she was a female.

* * *

Cathay and the other recruits stood outside the recruitment office waiting to be taken to the Jefferson Barracks, twelve miles south of St. Louis on the other side of the Mississippi River. Major Henry Merriam, the officer in charge of the St. Louis recruitment office, looked over the scraggly bunch of recruits in ill-fitting uniforms. Cathay admired the major's smartly pressed uniform with the burnished braid shoulders and recalled Colonel Benton who had taken her from the Johnson Plantation many years before. Was she going to be able to wear a uniform like that eventually?

"How many of you men have done military service?" Merriam asked. One or two men inched their hands up. Tall, slender Cathay stood slouched with her hands in her pocket. She did not raise her hand. She watched the Captain shake his head as he seemed to look at her.

I wonder if any of these former slaves will ever learn to stand tall and be proud of themselves as I was taught, Merriam thought.

As she thought it helped disguise her as a man, Cathay drooped her shoulders more. She hadn't had to take off her shirt as she changed into a blue uniform. She just stepped out of her overalls and into the uniform pants. Then her arms went into the jacket. Cathay was relieved that it was big. It made a good cover-up. The boots were big too, so she stuffed paper in the toes to make them fit. Her hat, called a *kepi*, fit poorly on Cathay's rough, kinky hair.

"You boys climb in over there," ordered a brawny sergeant, and herded her and the other recruits into a rickety wagon that rattled through the town as passersby stared. They thought it incredible to see so many colored soldiers in uniform on their way to Jefferson Barracks. Cathay clutched her military bundle close and resisted the urge to look around her. She wanted to keep as much to herself as possible until she could figure out her next move.

The barracks sat on a bluff across the river from St. Louis overlooking the town of Carondelet. On arriving, the sergeant made Cathay's group stand outside the barracks office. He took a sheaf of papers inside and returned with the barracks' commander.

There, at Jefferson Barracks, Cathay began her training as Private William Cathay, a member of Company A in the 38th Infantry Regiment, United States Army.

CHAPTER 21

Cathay was glad to see Jasper and Henry when she arrived at Jefferson Barracks. They tried not to show surprise at seeing her, but were anxious to find out how she managed her enlistment.

"I just did what you told me when we was in town," Cathay explained when they were alone. "I found some old clothes Miz Powers throwed away, and they fit just fine. I told her my mama was sick and I had to go take care of her. She didn't argue with me, but that gal, Daisy, didn't act too happy. I reckon she was gonna have to do for Miz Clara 'til someone else came along." Cathay shrugged and grinned. Jasper and Henry snickered.

She soon learned to follow the routine of the soldiers. Training as a real soldier gave her a sense of pride as she followed the maneuvers of the regiment.

* * *

Cathay marched with Company A in formation, often to the nearby town of Carondelet carrying backpacks and other equipment. She learned to shoot a musket, first standing still, then running. While she had traveled with the troops during the war, Cathay had never handled any of the weapons.

The first time she held her musket in her hands, it felt heavy and cumbersome. She loaded it like the sergeant in charge of weaponry instructed. Cathay had to bite the paper off the gunpowder cartridge without getting any gunpowder in her mouth. She poured the powder into the musket barrel and placed a metal musket ball inside. A long, metal rod pushed the musket ball tightly against the gunpowder. Loading the musket was tricky, because Cathay had to turn the gun upside down to load it with the handle resting on the ground. There was always a risk of the gunpowder exploding.

Once the musket was loaded, Cathay picked it up, pulled back on a hammer above the trigger to cock it into a firing position. When she pulled the trigger, a spark ignited the gunpowder and thrust the musket ball from the 40 inch barrel. Loading and firing the 10 pound weapon was not an easy task. Cathay practiced loading and shooting whenever she had a spare moment. The soldiers aimed at a target that held a bull's-eye. The first time she was able to hit the middle of the target, she yelled, "Whoopee!" The other soldiers around her laughed, but they cheered too. All the colored soldiers rejoiced when each one accomplished success.

Eventually, Cathay was able to load and shoot about three musket balls each minute. Later, she had to strike targets different from the bull's-eye. Sometimes the targets were moving. She hoped she'd never have to use her musket, but Cathay knew she could shoot as well as any of the other soldiers if she had to.

Under the command of Captain Charles E. Clarke, Cathay, Jasper, and Henry, thrived. While some of the officers bossed the colored soldiers like the overseers did when they were slaves, Captain Clarke treated them with respect. The soldiers of Company A were on their way to becoming well-trained.

* * *

Throughout the winter, many of the soldiers came down with various illnesses from simple colds and rheumatism to pneumonia. Cathay kept mostly to herself and stayed healthy.

But when the spring rains came in 1867, Private William Cathay became ill. She complained of aching pains in her back. Her eyes burned with fever and her head ached. Sore red spots appeared in her mouth and on her tongue. When she became dizzy and began vomiting, the sergeant in charge sent her to the infirmary. Three days later Cathay's face and arms broke out in a rash. The sores in her mouth worsened.

"You've got smallpox," the company doctor told Cathay. "That disease is contagious and we don't want any more of our soldiers catching it from you. You'll have to go to the regular hospital in East St. Louis, Illinois. They will place you in isolation until you recover."

He sent for a soldier who took Cathay in a wagon, down to the ferry and across the Mississippi river.

CHAPTER 22

The hospital was in a low lying area that was swampy and foul smelling. The spring rains caused the river to overflow, flooding the surrounding crowded city. Many people in the area caught the disease.

As Cathay glanced up from the wagon, she saw dirty stone covered buildings, clustered in grim looking groups; not at all like the clean, impressive-looking buildings she had seen when, as a slave, she landed in Washington City. While wanting to be treated for her illness, Cathay felt anxious, afraid of what kind of future awaited her in this miserable city.

The attendants lifted her on a stretcher, and placed her in an area of the hospital where she would be admitted to an isolation ward. Hospital workers rushed around her, but seemed to stay as far away from her as possible. Cathay groaned in pain as she awaited someone to care for her. Finally, a nurse approached with two orderlies. They wore long gowns covering their clothing, and masks covered their faces. The orderlies lifted Cathay's stretcher, and at the direction of the nurse, carried Cathay through dimly lit corridors to a ward full of smallpox victims, separate from patients with other illnesses.

The hospital beds were lined side by side in rows, but not all the patients were military. Cathay saw that some of the staff were not medical. They were other patients who were improving, who had developed an immunity to smallpox and could not get the disease again. The nurse inspected Cathay's face and arms and instructed the orderlies to cover her with a blanket. Later, a doctor arrived and gave the nurse orders of what medication should be given. A weak and exhausted Cathay finally drifted off into a troubled sleep.

Cathay's rash spread over her whole body. It formed bumps filled with a cloudy fluid called pus. Day after day,

Cathay drifted in and out of consciousness. At times she babbled deliriously, words that made no sense to others. Once when that happened, Rufus, one of the patient helpers, came over to her bed and listened to her mumbling. Cathay's swollen vocal cords made her voice deep and raspy. "Mama, Mama. Please don't make me. Don't make me go. I can't cook."

As she thrashed about in the bed, Cathay swung her arms around and kicked the sheet covering her. Flushed, her face was hot as though she had been standing before a baking oven. Her lips were parched, swollen, and cracked.

Rufus filled a basin with cool water.

"There, there," he crooned as he used a cloth to carefully sponge her face and neck. "You gonna be fine by 'n by." But Cathay hardly felt his kindly hands.

Rufus pulled the sheet lower on Cathay's body and opened her nightshirt to sponge her chest. His eyes widened.

"Oh, Lawd," he gasped. "This here soldier is a woman!"

Gently, Rufus replaced the sheet under Cathay's chin. He continued to pat Cathay's face with the wet cloth until she became cool and stopped mumbling. He wondered if anyone else had noticed. *If so*, he thought, *they were probably too distracted by their own condition to worry about Cathay.* Her feverish eyes stared blankly at Rufus. As he placed a wet sponge to her parched lips, he decided he would be the only one caring for her. He would see that the soldier got good care. She obviously wanted to be in the army and had somehow been able to join the military with her gender undetected. She deserved to have her chance. He would keep her secret; never tell what he had discovered.

* * *

Weeks went by and Cathay began to heal. The fever went down and her headaches came less frequently. The bumps hardened and formed thick scabs. Her voice remained permanently deep and husky. She noticed no one came near her but a kindly patient who brought her meals and medicine. He always left her when she needed to use the bedside privy. Cathay wondered if he discovered she was a woman. He never said.

Throughout Cathay's recovery, Rufus would chatter away as he cared for her. It was very comforting at first. Then one day Rufus asked "You been a soldier long?"

Cathay lowered her eyes. "I'm not sure," she muttered. The question made her feel uncomfortable.

Something about the way she answered made Rufus suspect she had no desire to talk, so he told her something about himself. "I never was in the army," he said. "I was in slavery on a plantation down near about Jackson County. My master called me Rufus 'cause-a my red hair. He was a good master, and when he got sick, he freed all-a us before he died. I headed north and found me a woman at the Johnson Plantation nearby Jefferson City. Her master said he'd allow us to jump the broom if I stayed on his plantation."

At the mention of the Johnson Plantation, Cathay looked up. Her eyes widened. She had never remembered seeing Rufus when she was growing up.

"I stayed and worked the fields awhile, but then I got restless," Rufus continued. "I had my freedom papers and I didn't want to do no slave work no more. My woman, Martha, was the Johnson's cook, and she wasn't free. I wanted her to come with me up north."

Rufus was quiet for a while. He seemed to be lost in his recollections. Cathay saw him get a far-away look in his eyes as he continued softly.

"I knew I could get her away along the freedom trail, but she was carrying our child. She didn't want to take a chance 'cause we would have had to travel mostly through the back woods and at night. I told Martha I would come later and get her and the baby." Rufus stopped talking as he saw the soldier turn her head away. He didn't want to tire her with his chatter. But he noticed she perked up a bit.

And Cathay *did* perk up. She began wondering if Rufus could be the father she had never known. *I sure wish I could ask him about those times he was at the Johnsons,* she thought.

A few days later, when Cathay was feeling stronger, she spoke to Rufus in her scratchy voice.

"Did you finally leave your wife?"

Rufus, happy to see Cathay willing to talk a little, told her some more about himself.

"I sho did. One night, I lit out for the trail with my papers. I had to be real careful 'cause I might get caught even with papers. Lotsa overseers wouldn't care about my papers and try to sell me back to slavers

I hooked up with abolitionists and finally got up to Philadelphia. But after the war started, I couldn't get back. I saw some people who got away from Jackson County later and heard tell I had a daughter."

Rufus bustled around doing his chores and shook his head from time to time, especially when he talked about Martha and the baby.

"Sure wish I coulda seen that little baby."

"What would you say if you'd seen her," Cathay asked.

"I don't know. But I know I would-a hug that little gal and wouldn't let nothing bad happen to her."

Cathay said nothing for a while. She seemed to be trying to weigh the things Rufus had told her.

"How old you think she'd be 'bout now?" she finally asked.

"Lemme see. 'Bout how old you be?"

"I think I'm 23 years old, give or take some."

"I 'spect she be 'bout your age. Wouldn't-a wanted her in that war though. Too dangerous. But I bet she'd make a nice wife for some fine young man."

Cathay stopped talking and turned herself away from Rufus. *I sure would like to find out if he's my father. But I can't take a chance on his finding out I'm his daughter. He might not like me being a soldier and then my army days would be over.*

Rufus also wondered where the young soldier came from. She was tall for a woman and he thought about his wife back on the plantation. Martha had been tall too. It wasn't often that he thought of his lost family, but caring for the young soldier made him remember. Rufus knew that William Johnson was reluctant to sell any of his slaves, but that was a long time ago. The war might have changed things. This young woman could even be his daughter.

CHAPTER 23

Several weeks later, a nurse came over to Cathay.

"You know this Rufus who's been taking care of you," she said. "He has been helping you and other patients, but he's going to be discharged soon. You're getting better and eventually you'll be able to return to Jefferson Barracks. You can help with the other patients now and that will help you get your strength back. Rufus has been a wonderful assistant and can show you what to do."

"Yes, ma'am. I'll do whatever I can to get well," Cathay answered.

As he showed Cathay her tasks, she continued to wonder if Rufus had discovered her secret. Most of their conversations were strictly about caring for the patients in the ward. However, when he saw how easily she learned to take over his tasks, he asked her what she did before she was freed.

"I helped take care the soldiers that got shot," was all she said. She said nothing more about any other experiences. Cathay remembered how she had nursed the wounded in battle. As she changed dressings on smallpox sores and sponged the patients' feverish bodies, she felt closer than ever to Rufus; a bond grew between them. She wondered if she dared tell him more about herself.

One day, as they were finishing caring for one of the patients, Rufus said, "Now that I'm getting better, I just might head to Jackson County to see if I can find my Martha. I was working my way back there when I came down with the fever. She be free now, and may not be on the Johnson Plantation. But them Johnsons kinda liked her, and she was a good cook. Maybe they kept her on."

Cathay turned away from Rufus as he spoke about her mama being a good cook. *Oh, Mama, I wish you could be here and listen to this man talk. Is he my daddy? Should I tell him about ME?*

Rufus interrupted Cathay's thoughts.

"What you gonna be doing when you discharged?"

Cathay's eyes filled with tears. She felt her heart thump so hard, she wondered if he heard it. How she wanted to tell Rufus who she was, but she remembered what he had said about not wanting his daughter in war. That was just where she would be if she continued to be a soldier. Even if she told him she was a woman, he might not keep her secret.

"I reckon I just keep on being a soldier," she answered. Sighing heavily, Cathay walked away.

Finally, the day came when Rufus readied himself to leave. Cathay wished she could write him a letter or send him a message like she did to tell Jasper about her going to Little Rock. But there was no messenger she could send with her special secret. Rufus shook Cathay's pox-marked hand and wished her well. As she watched him walk away, Private William Cathay hoped they might one day meet again.

And Rufus hoped the young female soldier would reach her heart's desire.

CHAPTER 24

Cathay continued practicing her nursing skills and showing her appreciation for the care she had received. Some of the patients did not recover, but she helped as many as she could. That also helped her regain strength just as the nurse had said. Cathay wanted to return to Company A as soon as she was able.

Meanwhile, Cathay's company, headed by Captain Clarke, had been ordered west to Fort Riley in eastern Kansas. They went to fill assignments accompanying wagon trains, guarding stagecoaches, and fighting Indians. Cathay had to be left behind.

Three months passed before Cathay was able to finally leave the hospital in East St. Louis. The scabs had fallen from the sores, and her heavily scarred face gave her a rugged appearance. Cathay didn't worry about the scars because she felt they probably helped her disguise. She wanted to look like a soldier. Her pox marked features gave her that look.

She reported to Captain Ward Hamilton at Jefferson Barracks.

"I don't see none-a my regiment, sir. Where'd they go?"

Captain Hamilton looked Cathay up and down. She had lost weight during her illness and her shoulders still slouched. Hamilton wondered if the skinny soldier would be able to serve Company A, as ordered, at their new post.

"Captain Clarke and Company A are now at Fort Riley, Kansas," said Captain Hamilton. "Your orders are to take the next train from Carondelet and join them." He reached under a stack of papers on his desk, pulled out a pouch, and handed it to Cathay. "Here are your orders. Don't lose them. When you get to the station, show them to the conductor on the train and he'll tell you what to do. Now go find your gear and get some food from the mess tent."

Cathay gathered her meager belongings and went to the mess tent. There she collected a lunch of gravy biscuits, salt pork, beans, and a small piece of beef. No doubt the lunch would be spoiled if not eaten by the time she reached Fort Riley. There was certainly no way to keep it fresh for three days. Cathay also took some hardtack to eat on the way. That would keep when the beef and salt pork was finished.

While Cathay was hospitalized, her bunk had been given to another recruit. She had nowhere to stay to wait for the train except at the station. She walked the familiar road down to Carondelet where she had marched many times on maneuvers. The spring-like weather made it possible for Cathay to rest outside the station until the train arrived. Cathay took several swallows from her canteen and ate a biscuit from her lunch. Then she spread her blanket on the ground beside a huge elderberry tree and settled down to wait.

The *chug, chug* of the engine and plumes of gray smoke and ashes announced the train's arrival later that morning. The conductor called, "All Aboard". Cathay showed him her papers and climbed the steps of the first passenger car. Since she was colored, she had to sit in the car closest to the engine. The soot and smoke settled there first. She watched the more privileged white passengers ride in cars farther back. There they would not get dirty from the ashes or choke on the fumes the engine belched out.

Even colored military had to follow the same rules of discrimination.

Still somewhat weak from her illness, Cathay welcomed the journey from Carondelet to St. Louis, Missouri, to Kansas City, Fort Leavenworth, and on to Fort Riley, Kansas. The journey took four days. It gave Cathay a chance to rest. No chores to do; no patients to tend; no marches or drills; just sweet, sweet rest.

During the journey, Cathay looked out the window at the familiar fields between Jefferson City and Jackson County. The landscape reminded her of slavery days that were behind her, and she thought again of her mama. Cathay wondered if Mama was alive and where she was. If she knew she was free, would she have decided to leave Miz Elizabeth and strike out on her own? She wondered if Rufus had found her and what he might have told her. Would they be able to figure that the soldier Rufus met in the hospital was indeed their daughter?

"What if Mama could see me now," she said to herself. "Wouldn't she be surprised!" Cathay said, chuckling softly. But a lump still came into her throat.

I'm not sure she'd like me posing as a man, she thought. *But that's just the way things is.*

CHAPTER 25

At Fort Riley, Cathay reported to Captain Clarke.

He looked much as she remembered him, tall and ruddy with kindly eyes. Of all the white officers she had encountered, Captain Clarke had gained her admiration the most. The colored regiments had white officers, who did not mingle with the colored soldiers except when they were giving orders. Even then they usually gave the orders through a colored sergeant in the regiment. While Captain Clarke sometimes gave orders through a colored sergeant, he often gave his regiment orders himself. That was one of the things Cathay liked about him.

"You look well rested, Private Cathay. Are you all recovered and fit for duty?" he asked as he greeted her.

Cathay gave Captain Clarke a brisk salute. "Yes, sir," she said.

"Well, take your gear and find your platoon on the other side of the fort. You'll find the group of tents where they stay."

The fort was not anything like Jefferson Barracks and unlike any of the forts she had seen in her travels with General Sheridan. It sat on a wide grassy plateau. A windy Kansas prairie sprawled around it at the edge of the western frontier. Fort Riley had no walls, no wooden fences; no stockade that usually protected the occupants from attacking Indians. Just a group of buildings surrounding an area for drills and parades. Some of these buildings housed soldiers.

However, not Company A. Since Cathay's company was a colored regiment, the soldiers were not allowed to stay in the same area with white soldiers. They were segregated from each other. They were not allowed to eat together or live in the same barracks. At each fort, the commanding officer decided whether the colored soldiers would camp on the fort grounds or outside. At Fort Riley,

Cathay went to a tent in a cluster that was arranged in a circle outside the compound. That was the only protection from Indians or the elements the colored soldiers could expect.

Cathay was happy to be reunited with Jasper and Henry. She described how she had met a patient that could have been her father.

"He was a freedman who said he jumped the broom with a slave named Martha who lived on the Johnson Plantation. Ain't that something? I kept wondering if he could be my daddy, but I didn't dare let on that I knew what he was talking about. He might've gave me away and then I wouldn't be able to join my regiment back here."

Jasper and Henry listened to Cathay's story in wonder. They knew she had lost her chance to ever know who the man was.

They began to describe events that occurred during the time they left Cathay in the hospital.

"We've been preparing to fight Indians," said Jasper. "Ain't seen none yet, but we knows they out there. We hear drums at night. So far they ain't attacked, but they just might."

"That red-headed General Custer up at the fort, he don't like those Indians a-tall. He don't like us neither, but he has to put up with us 'cause we's part of the army."

Henry seemed to be more confident than he was when Cathay had seen him earlier.

"Every day we goes out on patrol," Jasper continued. "Captain Clarke comes and gets us and say, 'Go march around and see what's out there.' Then we march a few miles around the place and come back. We goes up to the fort and work on the horses or clean up for the womenfolk. We gets our food up there, but they make us bring it back here to eat. Things ain't so clean here and there's bugs a-plenty. But we manage."

Cathay wasn't sure what she was going to be assigned to do, but she knew she didn't want to do laundry work anymore.

* * *

Each day Company A patrolled the perimeter of the fort. The soldiers saw no Indians. Cathay endured the disdain of the white women in the fort compound, but no one questioned her gender. She was just another colored recruit. She obeyed orders and said very little. She only talked when alone with Jasper or Henry. She enjoyed their company as they reminisced about old times on the plantation. Cathay spent more time with Henry because their duties were similar. Because Jasper had experience caring for horses before and during the war, most of his duties were at the stables working with the cavalry and their equipment.

One day, Cathay helped carry a basket of laundry for one of the colored laundresses in the fort compound. Some of the white soldiers pointed at her.

"Looks like that buck got himself a sweetie." The soldiers slapped their thighs and laughed loudly.

Cathay dropped her head and blushed, but no one noticed it through her dark skin. She put the laundry down and hurried off before the soldiers asked any questions.

Later, when Cathay was together with Henry, she mentioned what the soldier had said. Henry winked at her. "If you was gonna be anybody's sweetie," he said, "you would have to be mine." Jasper threw him a startled look as Cathay cuffed him in the back. Henry just laughed.

During the evening, when they were off duty, Henry, Jasper, Cathay, and the other soldiers in their Company would gather in a group around the compound telling stories, smoking pipes or chewing tobacco. Cathay usually had very little to say, but she watched them as they chewed some tobacco. They chewed and chewed and sent a stream of spit sailing across the ground.

Wanting to show that she was as manly as any of them, Cathay reached out her hand to Henry. "Let me have some-a that," she said. Henry and Jasper looked at each other with a question on their faces, but Henry handed her a piece of chewing tobacco and watched as she put it in her mouth.

Cathay chomped down on it and swallowed.

She coughed. She gagged. Her complexion turned a sickly forest green. To the sounds of laughter by the group, Cathay ran around to the back of their tent and vomited. Tears streamed from her eyes and she gasped for air. *Oh, Lord,* she thought. *I think I'm gonna die.*

A few minutes later, a smirking Jasper, peered around the corner of the tent. "You alright?" he asked. Cathay looked up at him sheepishly and nodded.

"What was you doin'?" asked Henry as he followed behind. His face showed a look of concern as he reached out and slapped her on the back.

Finally able to catch her breath, Cathay whispered.

"I thought I could act more like a man if I could chew and spit like you."

Jasper and Henry turned their heads and covered their mouths to keep their laughter from showing.

"Well, you don't eat tobacco," said Jasper when he got himself under control. "You just chew it and spit it out. I reckon you better just learn to spit."

"I reckon so," Cathay murmured, as she wiped her face and shuffled off to her bedroll.

CHAPTER 26

Company A was getting ready to move out. Jasper had just received the orders and hurried up to tell Cathay who was once again in the infirmary.

It seemed ever since Cathay had suffered with smallpox, her skin itched at the least little thing. She seemed to attract insects that bit her and caused bumps. They itched so much Cathay thought she would tear herself apart scratching. At times she would get sores that oozed and formed scabs. The fort doctor said she had scabies and put her in the infirmary for treatment.

This ain't hardly soldiering, Cathay thought. But again she had no choice. She had to stay there until the doctors discharged her. At least she didn't have smallpox again, and the scabies wasn't contagious.

Jasper spoke with the attendant at the infirmary and handed him a piece of paper. The attendant pointed toward the area where Cathay sat on the side of a cot with her elbows on her knees, holding her head in her hands. She had been in the infirmary a month, but the doctor said she couldn't be released until her skin healed.

"Cathay," Jasper called as he worked his way to her side. "We going to Fort Harker. You going too. You been discharged."

Cathay looked up, grinned, and breathed a big sigh. She was finally going to get to do some soldiering.

* * *

Fort Harker was larger than Fort Riley. Still under construction, it was a western Kansas outpost that housed many more soldiers. Cathay saw that it even housed some of the 10th Cavalry, colored horse soldiers that often escorted wagon trains and stagecoaches through Indian territory.

"I heard those soldiers be called 'Buffalo Soldiers',"
Jasper said to Cathay as they watched the 10th Calvary
members on their horses."They called that because they
look like them animals. They got wooly hair and brown
skin, so the Indians think they related." He laughed. Cathay
could see the longing in Jasper's eyes and knew he wished
he could belong to that regiment. She knew how much he
loved horses and yearned to serve in the army where he
could be riding them.

Cathay noticed the uniforms of the Buffalo Soldiers
were better than those of Company A, but not as new as
those of the white soldiers. Also their weapons and horses
were old and their equipment was often worn or damaged.

But that didn't matter. The 10th Calvary soldiers
were allowed to stable their horses nearer the fort so they
could ride out at a moment's notice whenever they were
called. They were known to be fierce fighters and
dependable protective escorts.

Company A and Cathay, once again segregated
from the fort, had to walk a mile to the fort parade grounds.
Wagon trains stopped and formed a circle between the
infantry compound and the cavalry quarters. But Cathay
had no problem going back and forth to drill and tend to her
chores. Her scabies had improved once she left Fort Riley.

The air at Fort Harker was clearer, and being farther away from the fort seemed to be the best thing for her.

CHAPTER 27

Cathay watched as a train of covered wagons rolled into Fort Harker. She knew the passengers were on their way West to find a new way of life. The wagon riders longed for open spaces away from the crowded eastern cities. Cathay realized traveling must not be easy, because usually the journeyers arrived dirty, weary, and bedraggled. They would stay at the fort only long enough to receive fresh water and supplies and then move on.

As the wagon train rolled uphill and circled into its usual formation, a woman and three children stumbled from one of the wagons. They dragged their tired bodies as if in a trance.

"Get over there and help those people." A man on horseback saw Cathay watching and yelled at her. The man, perhaps the wagon master, seemed to be in charge. Private William Cathay obeyed because she could see the woman needed help. The woman, and a boy, about seven years-old and not much bigger than the two little girls, struggled to lift a chest from the wagon.

When Cathay approached, the boy stepped back in fear. He dropped his end of the chest as Cathay reached for it. The woman noticed Cathay's uniform and reassured the boy.

"Don't worry," she said. "That's a soldier. See, he's wearing an army uniform."

Cathay grinned. She was happy to hear the woman identify her as a man. "Yes, ma'am. I'm Private Cathay. I can see you need some help unloading."

The bigger girl and the toddler plunked themselves by the side of the road. They looked up at Cathay with wide eyes, their faces tear-streaked and grimy.

A bucket and a keg hung from the side of the wagon. The bucket contained some water with a green scum covering it. When Cathay tried to get water from the keg, she found it was empty.

"You're gonna need water to drink and wash up with," Cathay said. "I'll fetch some." She took the pail and keg and trudged up to the pump near the parade grounds. There she scrubbed the bucket and filled the keg with fresh water. When Cathay returned with the water, the mother introduced herself.

"I'm Letty James and these are my children, Rebecca, Mary and Simon. We're heading West to join my husband. He's getting us land to settle on."

"I hear there's plenty land out there," said Cathay. "We gonna be moving out West later, too. Gonna join up with horse soldiers that're out there already."

Cathay gave the bucket to Letty James and returned the keg to the wagon.

"You set now," she said and turned toward the tent camp. "I best be getting back." Cathay waved to the children who raised their hands, and timidly returned the wave.

CHAPTER 28

The wagons stayed at the fort several days. That was unusual because most wagon trains left shortly after replenishing supplies and getting fresh water. Cathay was not surprised, though. Sometimes stale water caused the travelers to become diseased and they would have to stay longer. She knew there were many people with cholera and dysentery at the fort.

Cathay went about her usual chores, but didn't see the James family as she went back and forth. She saw several of the wagon train families and other riders and wondered where Miz Letty and her children had gone.

One night, Cathay heard a rustling outside the tent she shared with Jasper and Henry. Thinking it was Henry returning from guard duty, she ignored the sound. The tent flap opened and she saw Simon, Letty James's boy, standing outside. He was shivering and tears ran down his troubled face.

"What ails you, boy?" Cathay whispered as she pulled Simon into the tent. She grabbed a blanket and threw it around him.

"Lotsa people got sick. Mama too," Simon began. He hiccupped and tried to check his crying. "Now Rebecca's throwing up and got the runs. Mr. Jessup says he can't hold up the wagons for sick folks. We got no place to go."

Cathay's eyes showed her fear. What Simon described sounded like dysentery. She knew it was serious. Fort Harker infirmary was full of patients with contagious cholera and dysentery.   Many of the infected wagon travelers were denied treatment in the fort infirmary. They often died on the trails.

"Where's your mama now?" asked Cathay.

"She's in the wagon with Rebecca. But Mr. Jessup says he's gonna leave in the morning. If Mama's not able to travel, he's gonna use our wagon for supplies. Me 'n Mary don't know what to do."

Their talking woke Jasper who was asleep in the back of the tent. He sat up.

"What's going on?" he asked. When Jasper saw Simon, he jumped up and ran over to them. Cathay told him Simon's story.

"Can't we do somethin'?"

Jasper whispered harshly. "You know what'll happen if we gets caught with this white boy in our tent?"

Cathay looked down at Simon's anxious face. She knew they would be in trouble if they were caught. But she also knew how alone and helpless Simon must feel. Many times she had felt the same way and had been grateful for anyone kind and caring enough to rescue her.

"Maybe we can bring their things down here and Simon's family can rest in our tent 'til his mama gets better. I knows how to tend sick folks. None-a us caught nothing down here 'cause we been away from all that sickness up the fort."

"And you want to bring that sickness down here now!" Jasper paced around, waving his arms and opening and closing his fists in exasperation.

"It's just two people, Jasper," Cathay begged. "Simon and Mary ain't got it. If we sees they get clean water and bring them some-a our food, maybe they won't get sick. We can hide them 'til they gets well. Then we can send them back to get another wagon later."

Jasper looked into his cousin's pleading eyes and sighed. He knew she was tough, but there was a tender side to her also. She was so much like her mother, his Aunt Martha; tough, but tender. He hoped it would not give away her being a woman.

Jasper pointed over to his cot. "Go on over that cot and lay down," he told Simon. "We gonna think-a something."

Just then Henry came in from where he had been on guard duty. He was surprised to see Cathay and Jasper still up. When he spotted Simon, he gulped. Henry clapped his hand over his mouth and his eyes widened as he saw why Cathay and Jasper were awake. Jasper told him about the family's predicament and what Cathay wanted to do.

"I'll help anyways I can," he said, "but I sure don't wanna get sick. Anyhow it's gonna be tricky trying not to get caught."

Cathay looked at her dear friend gratefully. He always stuck with Jasper, but she knew she could always count on his help if she ever needed it. And here was where she needed it.

The three of them put their heads together and planned how to get the family to their tent without being seen. They knew they would have to work fast and carefully. The wagon train would be leaving the next day and they didn't want to be discovered moving anyone.

CHAPTER 29

Cathay and Jasper put on their jackets. Jasper shouldered his rifle and marched away as though he were relieving somebody on guard duty. Cathay crept to the James family's wagon and climbed in. She called softly.

"Miz Letty, it's Private Cathay."

Letty stirred on the pallet she shared with Rebecca. Mary was curled up on another pallet farther back in the wagon.

"Simon told us about your trouble and we gonna see if we can help. But you gotta leave this wagon so's we can nurse you and get you better."

Letty sat up. Her skin was pale and blue veins showed at her temples. Her dark, sunken eyes looked frightened at first, but she relaxed as she recognized Cathay as the soldier who had befriended them when they first arrived.

"We tried to go to the infirmary at the fort, but they turned us away," Letty whispered in a trembling voice. "They said they couldn't take wagon train people. The doctor gave us some medicine and sent us back here."

"If you don't mind we can take you and Rebecca down to our tents and hide you there 'til you better. Then you can take the next wagon train that comes along."

Letty shook her head. "I've got the children to care for. I can't leave them."

"They'll come too," said Cathay. "But they have to be quiet and not run around. If the sergeants see 'em, we be in big trouble."

"Why are you being so kind to us?" Letty asked.

"Simon said you needed help. We knows what being treated bad is. We was slaves before we was soldiers. Just because we been treated bad at times, no need to treat other people bad too. Every now and then, people treat us good. We remember how it feels."

Cathay helped Letty gather a few of the family's belongings. They roused Mary, and Letty cautioned her to be quiet. Cathay lifted Rebecca from the pallet. The toddler snuggled closely under Cathay's chin. Rebecca felt hot and was as light as a feather, even with a blanket wrapped around her.

As they moved toward the opening in the wagon, Jasper poked his head inside. "Ya'll better stay put. Here come more patrols." He turned and headed off toward the tent compound. Tramping feet signaled the patrols marching nearby.

Finally, it appeared to be safe. Jasper returned and helped Letty and Mary down from the wagon. He put his finger to his lips and motioned for them to follow him. They stole down the path to Cathay's tent. Rebecca moaned as they passed some other tents on the way and Cathay held her close, hoping no one heard her.

When they reached the tent, Henry had already prepared for the family. Letty and Rebecca shared Cathay's cot. Everyone else slept on pallets and bedrolls. By the time they were settled, the sun began to show a rosy glow as it rose. Cathay had no idea what the next days would bring. She prayed they would not be discovered.

* * *

Cathay strode up to the parade grounds. Mr. Jessup, the wagon master, called out to her.

"Where those people that were in this wagon?" He pointed to Letty's wagon.

"I think they was sick," said Cathay. "I reckon they went somewhere to get help."

"Well, good riddance!" Jessup yelled as he directed the wagon to be placed in his train.

Cathay continued up to the fort without a backward glance.

CHAPTER 30

Day after day Cathay nursed Letty and Rebecca.

Henry and Jasper took turns watching the James family whenever Cathay had to report for duty. Since she'd had experience working with the sick, she had been given infirmary duty to add to her other chores. That allowed her to get supplies to nurse the patients in her tent. Clean water and fresh food were the best remedies along with the medicine the doctor had given Letty.

Cathay hoped and prayed she herself wouldn't get sick again. She felt she'd already had her share of illness since joining the army, but didn't see how she could deny help for the toddler and her mother.

"What you gonna do with these chil'ren?" Henry asked one day. "You can't expect them to be quiet all day. We gonna be caught for sure." He kept twisting his hands and shaking his head. Cathay could see he was worried.

She had just finished giving Rebecca a sponge bath as Letty slept. Simon and Mary sat huddled in a corner of the tent. They watched and listened as the two soldiers talked. Mary and Simon had been quiet most of the time because they were frightened. The children had never been with soldiers before, especially colored ones. But as they became accustomed to being in the tent and saw how kind their hosts were, they were less afraid. Cathay knew the youngsters might become more active, restless, and noisy as the days went by.

"I'll think-a something," she said, as she swaddled Rebecca into a blanket and laid her back on the cot where she and Letty slept.

"Maybe we can give 'em some kinda game to play." Henry suggested.

Cathay stood up and stretched. "You mean like those string games we used to do back home?"

"Yeah, like cat's in the cradle."

Henry rummaged in his duffel bag and found a roll of twine. He pulled off a length of string, bit it, and tied the ends in a knot. Then he began to pull the string back and forth in a pattern. The children moved closer to Henry as his fingers formed a cradle web. Henry took Simon's finger, placed it in the web and pulled the web tight. Mary's face lit up in a smile. It was the first time Cathay had seen either of the children show any pleasure.

"Do some more, Henry, but don't get 'em laughing out too loud. We don't need to get caught now."

Cathay checked Rebecca under the blanket with her mother, and picked up the basin of water and wash cloths she'd used for the bath. She left the tent and carried the basin down the path where she emptied the water into a patch of shrubbery.

"Hey there, Will."

Cathay jumped at the sound of a voice behind her. She turned to see Clem Withers, another member of Company A. She hadn't noticed him following her down from the compound.

Clem leaned over Cathay's shoulder to see what was in the basin. "Why you got all them wet cloths?" Cathay had to think fast. She couldn't tell Clem about the family in her tent. But she knew she couldn't pretend to be sick either.

"I been helping tend some-a those folks up yonder at the fort," she said. "They so scared to catch something, they want me to clean these cloths down here. Wanna help?"

Clem cringed, shook his head, and began backing away.

"Uh, naw. Uh, that's alright. I got other things to do right now." He turned and scampered back up the path.

Once he looked over his shoulder to see Cathay wringing out the cloths. In his hurry, he tripped and almost fell. Cathay chuckled. She breathed a sigh of relief as she picked her way back to her quarters. She knew Clem to be a big gossiper. If he thought Cathay was helping take care of cholera patients, he'd probably spread the word and others would stay away from her. She thought that would be just fine, and whistled as she headed up to her tent.

CHAPTER 31

Letty and Rebecca began to recover. The children became happy and lively, but Henry kept them amused and quiet with string games and plantation stories. As Letty improved, she also taught them songs and read the Bible to them. Cathay brought Letty corn husks from the fort, and showed her how to make a doll for Rebecca. Cathay had almost forgotten about the dolls, because she never liked them. But she remembered a lot of the younger children on the plantation had played with corn husk dolls. She'd even made one for Miz Alice's girls who lived next to her and Mama in the quarters.

Jasper and Henry continued to keep watch for any members of Company A that might wander nearby. They also listened for news of wagon trains that were scheduled to arrive.

Just as Letty and Cathay thought there would never be an end to the family's three week isolation in the soldiers' tent, another wagon train rolled into the fort compound. The new wagon master galloped up to the fort office to report to Captain Clarke. Jasper, who always seemed to be stationed where he could get information, overheard the wagon master state he had space for anyone who wanted to join his train.

Jasper hurried down the hill where he found Cathay cleaning her musket outside their tent.

"Cathay, there's a new wagon master up at the fort. His name's Mistah Wright and he's younger and nicer than that Mistah Jessup. He got room for more people. Think we can get Miz Letty and her chil'ren with that train?"

Cathay leaned on her musket for a moment and closed her eyes in thought. Finally she straightened up."If Simon was to wander up the hill when the wagon master's round, he could ask about his mama and sisters joining them."

"Maybe Henry can take him up and make believe Simon lost his mama," Jasper suggested.

Cathay nodded. "Yeah. That's the way."

She and Jasper told Letty the plan. Letty instructed Simon on what to do when he went up to the wagon train. Meanwhile, she and the girls would mingle with the other families until Simon returned.

Later that evening, as the sun dipped behind the western clouds, Henry took Simon to the wagon compound.

"This here boy done got lost round our tents," Henry explained to the wagon master who was sitting on a broad bay mare near one of the wagons.

"Where's your mama?" asked Mr. Wright looking down at Simon from his horse.

Simon scuffed the ground with the toe of his shoe and dropped his head. "She's somewhere up at the fort," he mumbled.

"Well, hop up on my horse and we'll go see if we can find her." Henry boosted Simon up behind the wagon master who trotted off toward the fort.

"Don't worry," called Henry. "He gonna find your mama. Things gonna be alright." Then he hurried to their tent to get Letty and the girls. While Jasper stood watch, Cathay and Henry led the James family to the compound where the wagon train was camped.

"We'll bring your stuff up somewhere near the infirmary," said Cathay. "Act like you tryin' to find your child." She winked at Letty.

Letty looked at Cathay with tears in her eyes. "You've been so good to us. How can we ever thank you?"

Cathay and Henry turned and started back to their tent compound. "Just don't tell what we done. That'll get us in a peck a-trouble. Hope you find your husband out West."

Henry and Cathay walked down the path and never looked back.

Henry clicked his heels and skipped when they were close to their tent. "Whoo-wee!" he squealed. "We sure don't need nothing like that no more."

Cathay smiled. She had a good feeling about what they had done.

*   *   *

Letty clutched the hands of Mary and Rebecca and almost dragged them up toward the fort. She wasn't sure where to look for Simon, but she knew Henry had left him with the wagon master. And she knew the wagon master would be easy to find. The path to the fort was rocky, but the three struggled along the best they could in the waning light. On the way they spotted a man on horseback approaching them. Simon was sitting behind him.

"Oh, Simon, I've been looking all over for you. I'm glad this man found you." Letty hoped Simon remembered her instructions. She hoped he had not told the man where the family had spent the last few weeks.

"You need to keep track of your young'uns, ma'am. He tells me you need a space on our train. I think I can find some space, but you have to keep your stuff and children close to you. Don't go wandering off or we'll have to leave without you."

Simon slid from the horse and ran to his mother. Letty grabbed Simon and hugged him. "Thank the man, Simon."

Simon took Mary's hand as his mother scooped Rebecca into her arms. "Thanks," he said shyly.

"We'll get our things and be ready when you say," said Letty.

"Meet me at the compound in the morning. We leave at sunrise." Mr. Wright trotted his horse off down the path.

As the James family worked their way up to get their belongings near the infirmary, Letty gave Simon another hug.

"I'm so proud of you, son. I'll be sure to tell your daddy what a fine young man you've been."

They soon found a place to camp out near the wagons until it was time to leave.

Letty would always remember and have kind thoughts about those colored soldiers who had treated her family with compassion and generosity.

CHAPTER 32

$\mathbf{A}$ sense of satisfaction enveloped Cathay as she stood on the parade grounds and watched the wagon train pull out. The James family shared a wagon with another family and was on their way. Cathay had not been caught and was grateful to Henry and Jasper for their part in helping.

Cathay couldn't watch for long. The company sergeant's whistle blew and Cathay snapped to attention. White officers commanded the platoon, but the colored soldiers were drilled by one of their own members,

Sergeant Agee. Agee had run away from his slave master and joined the Union Army before the end of the Civil War. He was an experienced drill sergeant and Cathay felt proud that Company A drilled better than any other platoon in Fort Harker. Curious bystanders often watched as it followed its routine.

A horseman in a lieutenant's uniform rode up to the parading company. Sergeant Agee called a halt as the officer leaned down and spoke to him. The lieutenant gave him a piece of paper, and rode away.

"We got orders," barked the sergeant, waving the paper with their orders. "This here company's joining up with Major Merriam. He's taking over the 38th Regiment and heading to New Mexico. Get your gear and be back here at high noon. You dismissed."

Excitement galloped through the men of Company A as Cathay and the other soldiers broke ranks and scattered back to their compound. It seemed as though they had been at Fort Harker forever. The soldiers quickly dismantled their tents and piled them into supply wagons.

As Cathay prepared her bedroll, she remembered Major Merriam as the recruitment officer at the Jackson Courthouse when she joined the army. Was he the new commander? Cathay remembered his being tall with gray hair. She could almost see his stern looking eyes under bushy gray eyebrows. Cathay wondered if he would be kind and fair like their Captain Clarke who commanded Company A. And, would Major Merriam remember *her*?

Cathay hoisted the bulky bedroll and duffel bag and strapped them tightly to her back. Hooking the cartridge pouch to her belt, she slung a canteen and haversack across her shoulders. She picked up her musket and headed for the parade grounds. Cathay welcomed moving to another camp and hoped her duties would be more like what she saw soldiers do during the war.

Tired of lugging washtubs and laundry for the laundresses, she was sick of doing infirmary duty. She was glad to leave behind the infested Camp Harker, its cemetery overflowing with graves of cholera and dysentery victims.

As Cathay and the soldiers filled their haversacks with food from the mess tent; hardtack, jerky, and dried beans, Jasper came toward her from the stables. His face beamed with excitement as he related his news.

"I been assigned to the 10th Cavalry, Cathay. They gonna let me ride with them. This what I been wanting for a long time."

Cathay looked at her cousin with pride in her eyes. "I know, Jasper. We gonna miss you, but you gotta do what's best for you. Do Henry know yet?"

"I'm-a tell him soon's he gets his gear packed. Henry's gonna be alright. We're going on the same march, just in diff'rent parts. The cavalry will lead up ahead. This is gonna be a long march, Cathay," Jasper added. "Captain Clarke say make sure you got plenty water. Don't know when we find more."

Cathay nodded and waved as Jasper strutted off. She filled her canteen to the brim and wet a bandanna. She tucked it into her collar because she knew the days ahead would be scorching in the August sun. Then she went to find Henry. Cathay knew she would feel even closer to him in the coming days and weeks. He would be the only one who knew her true identity. Theirs would be a special friendship that she could not share with anyone else.

Company A pulled out at noon to join Major Merriam and the 38th regiment on the Santa Fe Trail. They were heading for New Mexico.

CHAPTER 33

The dust whipped around forming pillars along the Santa Fe Trail. Stretches of seared grassy plains lay ahead. Dust choked the soldiers, and their faces were grimy. Cathay's eyes smarted from the dirt and sun, but she didn't want to use the water she carried in her canteen to wash her face. Cathay needed every bit to drink until she could find a stream; or until they came upon a fort where the soldiers could refill their canteens.

The regiment had seen no Indians along the trail. The march was tedious and boring, but at one point along the trail Cathay's company escorted a Conestoga Wagon train to its next destination. Captain Clarke ordered his soldiers to march alongside, keeping a sharp eye out for Indians. The trail bosses rode horses ahead of the train. Although Cathay and the soldiers provided protection for the wagon train, some of its occupants were wary of the colored soldiers. So were many of the southern trail leaders who were still bitter about losing the war. They thought the colored soldiers should still be slaves.

The soldiers had been warned not to associate with the wagon train civilians in any way. Friendship with wagon train passengers would draw the soldiers' attention away from the escort duty they were along to perform. Company A's job was to be on the lookout for attacking Indians, so Cathay did not approach any of the travelers. She strained to see if there were any children in the wagons, but only saw men and an occasional woman.

Cathay thought of Miz Letty and her children, Simon, Mary, and Rebecca. What would have happened to them if she had not befriended them at Fort Harker? She hoped they reached Miz Letty's husband safely. *Families need ta be with families,* she thought.

Cathay shifted her bulky Springfield musket. Her equipment was heavy, but at least she felt more like a soldier as she scanned the surrounding land for signs of

Indians. She also tried to ignore her aching body with thoughts of Jasper.

Jasper's skill with horses finally had been noticed and he had been offered a transfer to the 10th Cavalry at Fort Harker. Although they were part of the march to New Mexico also, the cavalry was on the trail far ahead. Cathay was pleased that Jasper's dream had finally been realized, but how she missed his wisdom and companionship!

Only Henry remained a remnant from her plantation days. He was the only one left to guard Cathay's secret of womanhood. With Jasper gone, Henry's companionship became dearer than ever.

Private Cathay and the platoon treked along the dusty Santa Fe Trail, seeing tufts of grassland and goldenweed stretching for miles on either side. Occasionally, a cottonwood tree appeared in the distance. Its dull, ash gray trunk and leafless branches loomed high over the scorched plains. The soldiers marched where wagon wheels had gouged deep ruts making footing difficult. Also, they had to be ever cautious of snakes that often lay concealed, curled under rocks and road crevices, protected from the scorching sun. Cathay spotted an eagle gliding overhead. It seemed to search the land for prey in a careless little animal that dared to venture out of its burrow in broad daylight.

The platoon approached a herd of animals with wooly coats and small heads. Cathay saw a brush of black fur covering their humped shoulders. The huge animals shook the ground stirring up a cloud of dust as they ran.

"What're those animals out there?" Cathay asked one of the soldiers nearby.

"They're buffalo," the soldier answered. "They're what the Indians use for food and clothes and houses. They're why we get attacked. The Indians think we gonna kill 'em off. And I reckon they're about right. Lots of folks going West kill 'em just for sport."

So these are the animals the Indians honor so much, Cathay thought as she gazed in awe at the strange looking beasts. Buffalo. They were what the colored horse soldiers were named after. Buffalo Soldiers. The sight of the massive animals broke the monotony of the steady trek. They were so majestic that Cathay felt proud that the colored soldiers were named after them.

Overhead, the sky gradually grew dark, and ominous black clouds formed. A jagged flash of lightning and a burst of thunder erupted, signaling the approach of an oncoming storm. Captain Clarke had warned his troops that sudden storms were common in the plains. As the storm neared, Cathay watched as the buffalo herd became restless and began to huddle together in groups. They muddled round and round, scuffing and pounding the ground into a hole that would become a waterhole as soon as it rained.

Rain pelted down with a stinging force. Driving winds swirled it against the soldiers as they also huddled together. Cathay draped her poncho over her head and around her shoulders. She crouched with the other soldiers in her platoon as the cloudburst turned the dusty trail to thick mud. Some of the soldiers held out their pans to catch rainwater for filling their canteens. The cloudburst continued until the legs of Cathay's uniform soaked through and water seeped into her boots.

Henry, who had been marching near Cathay when the rain began, suddenly staggered and toppled forward. Cathay knelt down, turned him over, and shook him. Henry looked up at her with unseeing eyes.

"What's the matter, Henry?" Cathay asked, shaking him again, but Henry just groaned.

Cathay yelled to one of the soldiers nearby. "Get the sergeant. This here man's sick."

Henry's body trembled and his teeth chattered as the rain poured down on him. The soldiers held their ponchos over him, trying to shelter him from the torrent as much as possible. But they hadn't been prepared for the sudden storm or for Henry's collapse.

Sergeant Agee arrived with two of the messengers. "Get that man over the side of the road and put up a tent," he ordered.

The wind swayed the canvas and the rain caused the soldiers' hands to slide as they struggled to erect a shelter for Henry and Cathay.

Finally, a somewhat shaky tent was erected in the muddy ground. Soldiers lifted Henry onto blankets they had laid out. Cathay toweled his face and neck the best she could and loosened his jacket as he gasped for air. Henry's wool uniform, standard issue for the soldiers, provided a little warmth, but it was wet. His Adam's apple bobbed up and down with each breath. The chills continued.

Cathay knelt beside Henry and continued to wipe his face. She heard a stir from outside the tent as Captain Clarke strode in. She saw that although his poncho covered his official uniform from his head to the top of his boots, water still spilled from the brim of his hat

"What's wrong with this man?" he asked.

Cathay looked up from her kneeling position. "Don't know, sir. He just fell over and started shakin'."

"Has he been near any of those wagons where there was cholera?"

"Maybe so, sir. Hard to say. We been guarding wagon trains now and again since we started this here march, but we ain't really had no contact with those people.

Cathay knew chills and fever were some of the symptoms of cholera, but Henry hadn't shown any of those signs earlier. They were all tired during the long march and some of his symptoms could be exhaustion. She knew he had never been as strong and healthy as Jasper, even when they lived back on the plantation. She wondered if Henry could have been infected by the James family, but that seemed too long ago to matter.

"Get this man on a stretcher and we'll set up camp the first time we see a decent spot." Captain Clarke addressed Sergeant Agee who stood nearby, and then strode out of the tent.

The buffalo herd shifted with the sudden activity of the soldiers. The storm began to lessen, the wind died down, and the rain decreased to a soft drizzle. The herd lined up and moved away in a single file. Cows hovered over their calves, urging them along with the others. Cathay hovered over Henry.

"Hang on, Henry," whispered Cathay as she stood up. "We gonna get you some help soon." A slight groan was all Henry uttered.

CHAPTER 34

The platoon marched for ten miles before they came to a suitable place to camp. The rain had stopped, but left the air damp and thick with fog. The soldiers slipped and slid on the muddy trail. Those soldiers who carried Henry found their footing especially difficult with the weight of the stretcher. All the uniforms were wet with sweat under the rubbery ponchos. There was little chance of them drying in the humid air.

Cathay cared for Henry, while the rest of the soldiers set up camp. Some of them cast wary glances over their shoulders as Cathay unbuttoned Henry's uniform jacket and continued to wipe his face and neck. They knew Cathay and Henry had been on the same plantation during slavery, and that she had attended the sick at Fort Harker. The soldiers also knew she had treated wounded soldiers in the war and were satisfied to leave Henry in Cathay's care.

For two days the platoon stayed at the campsite. They moved around, fixing meals, drying out, and cleaning weapons during the day, and performing guard duty at night. They were lucky only because no more flash storms arose while they camped.

Someone kept a fire going so Henry could be warm, but he became weaker and weaker. He began to vomit and at times he was delirious and groaned as if in pain. Cathay gave him sips of water the soldiers collected from the cloudburst. She soothed his feverish body with damp cloths. That was the best she could do since she had no medicine. She tried to soothe his mind with encouraging words.

"Come on, Henry. You know how much we needs you. You my dear friend from plantation days. "Remember how we played around the quarters? How you helped Miz Letty's children with those string games? You gonna be all right. Just hang on."

While Cathay wasn't sure what kind of sickness he had, she prayed Henry would recover soon. She also prayed he would not reveal her identity in his delerium.

Although the soldiers rested for a short time, it still was not enough time for them to recover their energy. It made them jumpy to have one of their platoon sick with a mysterious illness. They stayed as far away from him as they could. The soldiers hoped Henry did not have cholera, as they remembered the many bodies they had buried at Fort Harker.

Finally, Major Merriam sent Captain Clarke a message that the group could not delay any longer. The march would have to resume. As soon as they arrived at Fort Zarah, Kansas, which was on their way, they would leave Henry to get medical attention. Fort Zarah had an infirmary and the wagon trains' travelers often rested there.

The members of Company A broke camp. Cathay helped secure Henry on a stretcher and the march began again.

*   *   *

On their arrival at Fort Zarah, some of the soldiers of A Company left Henry at the infirmary. Major Merriam had sent orders that the platoon should join the rest of the regiment that was farther ahead away from Fort Zarah. He wanted his troops to have very little contact with places where the wagon trains camped. Major Merriam realized that the people who traveled in the wagon caravans were those who spread the disease. He didn't want his soldiers exposed to any of them.

Cathay wished she could stay with Henry, but knew she had to continue with her platoon. Hurriedly, she said goodbye as she left him..

"I hope I sees you again soon, Henry. You supposed to join us when you gets better. You knows you my only dear plantation friend."

As Henry waved weakly, Cathay's heart ached with a deep sadness. She was leaving the only special friend who knew her identity as a woman. She knew she would have to be more careful than ever. She would have to keep her own counsel.

And her own secret.

CHAPTER 35

Cathay and the other soldiers in Company A had looked forward to settling at Fort Zarah for a much needed rest. They could not relax at the campsite right after Henry collapsed. Anxiety over Henry and his illness, and camping out in wet clothing increased their discomfort. Two days only gave them a break from the storm, caused them to be tense, and caused tempers to flare.

Furthermore, Major Merriam ordered them to leave Henry and march forty miles farther to join the battalion at Fort Larned, Kansas. Cathay noticed two more soldiers shuffling along the side of the road. They looked like they were ready to drop. They almost looked like Henry did when he collapsed and that worried her. Although Cathay was weary too, she mustered up enough strength and nerve to approach Sergeant Agee, the leader of the platoon.

"We need to rest more'n two days, sir. Them soldiers near about dead." Cathay pointed to her struggling companions.

The sergeant, who didn't want any of the soldiers in his group to appear soft and sluggish, stomped over and prodded the soldiers with his rifle.

"Get along there," he barked. The soldiers attempted to stand straighter and pick up their pace a little. But as soon as Sergeant Agee walked away they resumed their shuffling. After a few more miles, both collapsed.

Cathay lifted the arms of one of them around her shoulders and dragged him along. Another soldier assisted the other one. They strained as they shifted the exhausted soldiers' gear from side to side while struggling with their own equipment. After a mile or so, other members of the platoon came to their relief.

When Company A reached Fort Larned, a messenger from the fort commander met the soldiers and told them they must camp several hundred yards away from the fort. The fort commander had received the rumor that the soldiers were spreading disease.

Again the colored regiment was not allowed the comfort of a fort.

* * *

Cathay pulled off her boots and inspected her swollen feet. Huge blisters covered the soles. Both feet were bruised and sore, but her right foot was raw and sticky with blood. Her shoulders ached from carrying her gear and assisting other soldiers on the trail. The fort commander had at least provided the regiment with enough water to bathe their lacerations and fill their canteens. He also sent several rolls of bandages. Cathay used one to wrap her right foot until it could heal.

Nearby, Cathay overheard some of the soldiers grumbling.

"They don't let us settle down in none-a these forts. They think we bring on sickness."

"Naw, that ain't it. They don't want us because we colored. They treat us like we still slaves."

"Well, we not slaves no more. We part of this here army. We just as good as they is and can fight as well as they can."

Cathay wanted to join in the conversation and say none of them did any fighting. They just built fences and did guard duty. They just marched and paraded. They just carried equipment and cleaned up campsites. They really didn't do much that she could call soldiering.

But she kept quiet. Since they'd left Henry, Cathay was afraid she might say something that would reveal her as a woman. Remembering her tobacco chewing experience with Jasper and Henry, Cathay had acted as hard as the other soldiers. She'd practiced chewing and spitting tobacco whenever she was alone. She no longer swallowed it and could spit a good distance through her teeth. That helped to prove her manliness with the other soldiers. When Cathay was in their presence, she often accepted a plug of tobacco and chewed and spit with the best of them. She even swore every now and then. *Don't want nothing to change their minds about me now.*

The weather was Cathay's best ally. None of the soldiers bathed and they slept in their clothes during the cold nights. Cathay's jacket was usually buttoned up to her throat. When the sun was hot and she had to remove her jacket, a blousy shirt covered up her small breasts. So far no one suspected that Private William Cathay was really Cathay Williams, female soldier.

CHAPTER 36

Private Cathay moved steadily along the Santa Fe Trail with her platoon. She watched the land as it changed from the dried grass of the prairie in Kansas to the mountains of New Mexico. Cathay remembered the mountains she'd crossed after Colonel Benton took her and the other Johnson slaves from the plantation. Unlike the Arkansas Mountains, where the clouds hung heavy, seemingly to the ground, these snowcapped peaks towered into almost cloudless skies. The brisk, cold air surrounded streams where clear water flowed, water plentiful with fish. Thick forests covered the mountainsides.

Major Merriam's troops moved camp every few days. This strategy kept the soldiers free from the scourge of the disease, but kept their morale low. After traveling 500 miles in Kansas from Fort Harker, past Forts Zarah, Larned, and Dodge, Cathay and the members of Company A finally spotted a welcome sight. They saw what was to be their final destination: the United States flag waving over Fort Union, New Mexico in the distance.

In spite of their weariness, the soldiers cheered and broke into song. Their journey had come to an end. This was to be their final destination. Everyone stepped livelier as they surged toward the fort.

* * *

Three uniformed cavalrymen galloped from the fort toward the regiment, and approached Major Merriam as he halted his troops. One of them handed the major a packet of orders. Merriam read the first few pages. His face turned red with rage and his cheeks rounded like a puffer fish. He looked as if he was about to explode. The major shook his fist at the uniformed riders and his usual calm commanding voice erupted in indignation.

"This is an outrage," he screamed. "These men have traveled hundreds of miles to reach this fort. They deserve to enter as much as anyone there." The cavalrymen reined their horses around at the verbal attack, as another man clothed in buckskin rode up.

"Follow me," said the rider. "I'm the scout the commander sent to lead you to the quarantine camp down yonder. You'll have to set up camp by the creek until you get more orders."

Major Merriam spurred his horse and it reared, matching Merriam's defiance. The major turned to follow the scout, his face still contorted with anger beneath a shaggy beard. He commanded the regiment about face. Merriam resented his troop's being kept from the comfort of the fort since they were no threat of disease.

However, Cathay soon found the Fort Union quarantine camp beside Ocate Creek was probably the best situation Company A had encountered after their long march. Although they had to sleep in bedrolls on the ground, she and the other soldiers did not have to do their usual chores. While at the quarantine camp, they were able to relax and rest weary, aching bones; their blistered feet soon healed; they enjoyed time off from menial labor, guard duty and patrols.

Cathay had one problem with the quarantine camp. There were no large tents at the camp, and no outhouses like there were at the forts. Cathay had always found some private place when she had to go to relieve herself and take care of her bodily functions. The men peed and crapped wherever they found bushes for cover.

Henry or Jasper had stood watch whenever Cathay had to perform any of her bathroom duties. But at Fort Union, Cathay had no one to stand watch. She was on her own. The men stood to pee, but Cathay had to search for a shielded place to squat. Occasionally, she relieved herself in the creek, but in an emergency, she couldn't get to the creek in time.

"Why you always sit down to pee?" one of the soldiers asked Cathay one day.

Cathay snarled. "Mind your business. Ain't none-a your business how I does mine." She glared at the soldier and stomped off, pulling her pants up along the way. She would have to figure out some method of peeing when she was standing.

The next time Cathay had to relieve herself, she sidled over to a tree near the edge of the camp. She opened up her pants and lifted up her leg like the dogs did. She let out a stream of pee that shot forward like the male soldiers'. As long as Cathay could find enough cover, she knew this position would work in case anyone happened to be watching. Then no one would question her again. Her pants got wet, but often, the men came back with their pants wet. No one would suspect anything.

It was three weeks before the quarantine was lifted. The fort commander finally allowed Major Merriam and the 38th infantry regiment to enter Fort Union. Cathay stood straight and tall in the neat and orderly formation of the 38th Regiment as Company A marched into the fort with Major Merriam and Captain Clarke at their head. They marched with pride as if they had won a great military victory.

The fort commander had finally realized what Major Merriam knew all along. The colored troops did not spread disease!

CHAPTER 37

After relaxing at the quarantine camp, Cathay and her companions were rested and ready to resume their military duties. She worked alongside the men of Company A, performing the same guard duty, stringing telegraph wires, cleaning camp sites, transporting water, repairing fences and walls, and other mundane duties around Fort Union that the officers commanded.

Spanish women and other colored women at Fort Union performed the laundry work so it was not one of

Cathay's duties. *I sure did enough of those jobs with General Sheridan's army,* she thought.

The people at Fort Union represented a mixture of Spanish and Indian cultures that were friendlier to the colored soldiers than Cathay had seen at other camps. They noticed how disciplined, hardworking and punctual the soldiers in the 38th regiment were. Frontiersmen began calling the colored infantry "Buffalo Soldiers" also, the name the Cheyenne gave to the 10th Cavalry. Knowing the respect Indians had for the buffalo, the animals that provided much for the Indians' needs, the colored infantry and cavalry accepted the title of Buffalo Soldier with pride.

Cathay heard that the Indian encounters with the colored cavalry showed they were extremely courageous. They exhibited a fierce determination whether fighting Indians, pursuing and capturing frontier outlaws, or protecting railroad construction crews. Military records later revealed fewer desertions from Buffalo Soldier regiments than white regiments.

Private Cathay still had to work in the kitchen, stoking fires, and scrubbing floors. But she no longer cooked. Cooking was usually done by Spanish occupants. At times she went on patrol or helped the cavalry soldiers clean out the manure from the stables. She and the other colored soldiers also performed many of the dirty chores that the white soldiers refused to do.

Occasionally, Cathay would talk with one or another of the civilian servants, but she preferred to keep to herself or with her platoon members. Once she'd had a conversation with Esperanza Garcia, one of the Spanish cooks. She informed Cathay about the activities at Fort Union.

"Sometimes we have fiestas with music and dancing. The colored soldiers join in or just watch if they want to. You should come."

"Oh, I don't know. I don't dance and most times I'm on guard duty."

Esperanza stopped peeling potatoes and threw her long, black braid over her shoulder. "Everybody needs fun sometime," she answered, smiling. "You don't have to work *all* the time."

Esperanza winked.

Cathay recognized Esperanza's flirting. She knew the cook thought the tall slender private was a man who might take her to one of the dances.

"I don't have no time for parties," Cathay growled. "My soldier jobs keeps me too busy or too tired." She hurried away before Esperanza could say any more.

One night, as she listened to the music that floated over the regiment's quarters from the parade grounds, Cathay decided to wander near one of the fiestas Esperanza talked about. She approached the area where the music, dancing, and merrymaking took place. Cathay stood in the crowd with some of her platoon and watched the festivities.

The music reminded her of the few times the slaves had a shindig back on the plantation. Usually it was when a couple jumped the broom to marry; or when Mastah William celebrated something special like his birthday. There'd be a huge party at the big house and the servants would get some treats to take down to the quarters. The slaves would be allowed to celebrate too.

Cathay longed to join in the dancing like the frontiersmen and the Spanish women, but she was afraid someone would recognize she danced more like a woman than a man. Fiesta times made her long for her true identity. They made her yearn for Henry or Jasper when she could relax and be herself. So she just clicked her fingers and patted her foot to the melodies of the guitar and rhythm of the tambourines.

Suddenly, Esperanza, who was swaying and switching around the square, spotted Cathay at the edge of the crowd.

"Hey, Private Cathay," she called. "Come over here and dance with me."

Private William Cathay stiffened. Startled and panic-stricken, she spun around and stumbled through the crowd. The soldiers, who stood nearby, laughed.

"He's so scared a-women," one of them said. "I'll dance with you." And the Buffalo Soldier skipped over to Esperanza and began hopping around the circle with her.

Cathay sprinted all the way back to her quarters. Hot tears stung her eyes. She trembled as she realized she had almost given herself away by remembering the simple pleasures from her childhood. *From now on, I jus' drown myself in my reg'lar chores; clean up roun' the kitchen; go on patrol; work on the fences; muck out the stables; anything the sergeant orders me to do. No more rememberin',* she thought.

A friendship with Esperanza would have been welcomed, but Private William Cathay knew she couldn't take that risk. She would have to be just as cautious with the women as she was with the men.

Despite the hard work and lack of close friends, Cathay liked being at Fort Union. For once the food was more than the usual salt pork and dried beans. Cathay had never tasted elk meat or goat's milk. She discovered a love of Spanish cooking. Corn and beans spiced with chiles and tomatoes tasted different from the way they had been prepared on the plantation. Tortillas were very different from buttermilk biscuits. Chorizos, refried beans, and enchilados were her favorites.

Cathay followed the comings and goings of the busy activities at the fort. Wagon train passengers and frontiersmen brought news from the other forts and from places back East. Merchants sold goods and traded with friendly Indians. Children played games around their wagons and reminded Cathay of Simon and Mary and Rebecca James.

She loved the wide valleys, snow-capped mountains, vast grazing lands and tall cedars. After two wonderful, serene months at Fort Union, Cathay felt at home at the ideal post.

And then the order came.

Again.

Company A must move.

Again.

AGAIN.

Sergeant Agee marched through the Buffalo Soldier's quarters barking commands.

"Get your gear together. We're moving to Fort Cummings."

CHAPTER 38

The Buffalo Soldiers began grumbling as they showed their discontent. Cathay heard more of the complaints about the way the colored soldiers were being treated.

"Here we go. Moving again."

"We going to another place like we some gypsies or something."

"Soon's we get someplace where we can live better, they just jerk us up and move us away."

While Cathay disagreed also, she kept her thoughts to herself. She did not want to be treated as some soldiers who disagreed with orders from their officers were often punished. They were placed in the stockade, or given extra guard duty. Sometimes they had their rations cut, or were given some unpleasant task as cleaning outhouses. Cathay knew orders were to be obeyed, not questioned. So she followed her orders without complaining.

After Cathay's previous treks, she was used to the forty or fifty pounds of equipment strapped to her back and shoulders. Her musket and cartridge pouch felt as much a part of her body as her arms and hands. Although disappointed having to leave the tree clad mountains and lush grazing lands surrounding Fort Union, Private Cathay still resolved to do the best soldiering at her new post. After all she'd been through, she felt this was just another challenge to overcome.

Yet, she was not prepared for the harsh desert crossing ahead. The dry, hard ground, unlike the grasslands of Kansas and the tree covered mountains of Northern New Mexico, displayed plants vastly different from those she knew around Fort Union. Yucca and cactus with treacherous thorns replaced the lush shrubbery she had grown to enjoy. Cathay saw creosote bushes and gnarly mesquites instead of the cool pines and aspens. She slept fitfully even when she was exhausted. Gila monsters and scorpions were new to her. The red ants and tarantulas differed from the ants and spiders she knew in the east. Always afraid of rattlesnakes, Cathay jumped whenever she heard scurrying nocturnal animals scampering over her bed roll.

Throughout the night, coyotes sang to each other, their eerie howls echoing across the moonlit desert. The soldiers in Cathay's platoon had to be on the constant lookout for mountain lions on the prowl. Marauding Apaches, camped in nearby canyons, threatened to raid the platoon whenever it settled for the night. Furthermore, to reach Fort Cummings, the troops had to cross the Rio Grande River; the river that began in southern Colorado and snaked its way across New Mexico to the Mexican border.

As they approached the Rio Grande, Sergeant Agee, still the Company A leader, informed his platoon, "This river too deep most places. We'll look for a place where we can wade if possible. If we don't find that spot, we just have to swim across. So be prepared."

Cathay listened and thought, *And if I drown, that sure be the end-a my soldierin'.* But she trudged along the bank of the river with the other members of Company A, looking for a shallow area.

The soldiers finally arrived at a crossing spot where they could clearly see the opposite shore.

Sergeant Agee constantly barked orders. "Find shrubbery and anything that's strong enough to make a raft to float our gear and weapons across. Wrap your guns in your ponchos so they don't get wet."

Cathay wrapped her musket in her poncho and placed it with the other weapons on the rafts. While several soldiers guided the raft across, she and her other companions began to wade into the river.

It was early morning, barely sunup, and the air still held the chilled night temperature of the desert. As she ventured into the dark, forbidding depths of the Rio Grande, Cathay remembered one of the songs the slaves used to sing back on the plantation.

Jordan River, chilly and cold,

Chill my body but not my soul.

Cathay thought. *This here river chills my body and my soul.*

The muddy, spongy riverbed sucked her feet with each step she took as Cathay waded farther and deeper into the river. If Private Cathay had been shorter she would have had to swim because the water already reached her chest. But she could see that her companions ahead were no deeper, so she plowed on toward the far shore.

Suddenly, Cathay's stepped into a hole in the riverbed. As she tried to gain her footing, she slipped and toppled forward. Her head and shoulders dipped beneath the surface of the water. Cathay thrashed about trying to regain her balance. She swallowed a mouthful of the murky water as she sank. She held her breath, but her lungs felt as though they would burst.

Just as Cathay felt she would have to breathe and would surely drown, someone grabbed her jacket and lifted her out of the water. But not before water went up her nose and into her ears. She felt her ears pop as she gulped air. Private Ben Mosley had been following a short distance behind Cathay. He saw her stumble and hurried to her rescue. Mosley half carried, half dragged Cathay to the shore.

As they neared the shore, the platoon gained a foothold on firmer ground. Cathay surged forward and landed face down in the mud of the river bank. Her breath came in short gasps and she vomited some of the Rio Grande and bits of silt she had swallowed. All around her the other members of Company A were lying on the ground or shedding their wet clothing. Private Mosley crawled over to Cathay and began to remove her jacket.

Cathay pulled away from him. She struggled to sit up and hugged her wet arms across her chest.

"Leave me alone," she whispered. "Go away. I take it off myself later."

Private William Cathay continued to hug herself and rocked back and forth in the mud. While she knew she showed some ingratitude for Mosely's kind gesture, she feared his discovering her gender if he attempted to remove her clothing.

Mosley shrugged, stood up, and moved away to help someone else.

CHAPTER 39

In the heart of Apache country, Fort Cummings was a new compound built to protect the area from hostile Indians. It was fortified with mesquite wood and a red clay called adobe, native to the area. When mixed with straw and certain minerals and baked in the sun, the adobe bricks made strong, defensive walls.

Cathay wished she could have still been stationed at beautiful Fort Union. There the cool, fresh air and green forestry contrasted greatly with the parched, barren desert of Fort Cummings. The desert dry air burned her eyes during the day and made her throat scratchy at night. But since Fort Cummings was to be the home of her regiment, she at least appreciated the fact that Captain Clarke had been assigned the fort's commander.

The main job of Private Cathay's platoon was to collect wood for fuel. The commanders assigned small groups of men called *details*, from each platoon to perform certain tasks. Since trees were not plentiful in the area, one of the groups had to travel several miles from the fort to find the firewood. While a soldier patrolled, the rest cut trees and chopped wood. A soldier from the fort brought a mule drawn wagon to haul the wood back.

As trees in one place became completely eliminated, Cathay and her detail searched farther and farther from the fort. Often the detail stayed overnight, because they were more than a day's travel away.

During one session, Cathay was on patrol while the other soldiers worked cutting trees. As she marched around, keeping on the lookout for Indians, she found herself moving in ever wider circles. Soon she realized she had lost sight of the group in her work detail. Cathay tried to retrace her path, but the entire desert looked the same. As she wandered, daylight faded and the moon rose.

Private Cathay was lost.

The desert temperature dropped and with only her wool uniform and waterproof poncho for warmth and the moon for light, Cathay knew she'd better not search for her companions until the next day.

A short way ahead, a cluster of buttes loomed. She knew these isolated hills with smooth sides had cave-like crevices where she could find shelter. Cathay crawled up the side of a butte and into one of the crevice openings. She wrapped her poncho around her and huddled close to the stone.

Night critters scuttled around her and she feared the crevice would contain bats. Cathay hated bats. Also, she wondered if the cave might be the den of some desert creature, but it was the best protection she could find. It would have to do. In the distance she heard howling songs of wolves or coyotes. She trembled as she thought of mountain lions and hoped she would not encounter one. Although shivering from the cold, she remained as motionless as she could. Watching the moon rise higher in the sky and the twinkling stars, she began to nod.

Eventually, Cathay fell asleep.

A strong, rancid odor and a grunting sound woke Cathay at dawn. Below the crevice some pig-like animals sniffed and rooted among the brush. The peccaries were searching for choice vegetation that grew at the base of the rocks. The sun shone on the butte as she watched the strange animals.

Suddenly, a shadow glided over her. She stiffened and her attention moved from the foul smelling animals to her musket nearby. As she reached for it, a knife whistled past her ear and two tall Apaches appeared above her. One of them grabbed the musket and pointed it at her.

Cathay knew there were Indians in the distant hills. Often she heard their drums. Once or twice they raided livestock that wandered outside the fort, but none had attempted to attack the well-fortified garrison. She knew other wood collecting details had reported seeing Apaches from time to time, but this was her first meeting.

With the musket pointed toward her, Cathay expected the Indian to shoot her. Instead, his companion bent down and grabbed her poncho. He wrapped it around his shoulders and spoke in a language Cathay did not understand.

The Indians wore deerskin shirts and breechcloths that looked like aprons with a front and a back. Leggings attached to moccasins made them look like boots. The top of the leggings were rolled downward to make a pocket. Cathay thought the pocket was where the Apache had kept the knife that he had thrown at her. Each Indian wore a wide colorful headband around his dark, shiny, shoulder-length hair. Their ruddy brown faces were smooth and beardless.

The Apache, who grabbed Cathay's poncho, reached out and rubbed her face. His long, rough fingers scratched her. He uttered something to his companion. Cathay slapped his hand away as she struggled to her feet. If she was going to die, she would die standing tall as a brave soldier should.

The Indian's eyes widened with surprise at the gangly private's height and spunk. With the musket still pointed at her, the Indian grabbed Cathay and dragged her from the shelter. He pushed her downward away from the butte and forced her ahead of him, continually prodding her back with the muzzle of the musket.

Wonder why he don't shoot me, Cathay thought. Were the Indians going to take her back to their camp? What would they do then? Would they torture her? Would they scalp her in revenge like some of the white frontiersmen were known to scalp Apaches they captured?

The Indians pushed Cathay toward two horses that stood at one side of the butte. In the distance they spotted the rest of Cathay's detail approaching with the mule drawn wagon used to carry loads of wood. All the soldiers had their muskets and rifles drawn and pointed at the Indians. One of the soldiers fired a warning shot into the air.

The Indian with Cathay's musket scrambled to his horse taking the gun with him. The other Apache yelled a high-pitched scream, threw Cathay's poncho and her to the ground, and mounted also. Both Indians galloped away, their whoops and screams echoing in the distance.

The detail of soldiers came closer. Cathay stumbled toward them, relieved to be alive.

Why had the Apaches spared her? Were they puzzled by her colored skin, so similar to their own? Was it true that the Indians respected the Buffalo Soldiers, so named by their Cheyenne brothers? Or did they suspect Cathay was a woman? She could only wonder.

CHAPTER 40

The officers assigned Cathay and the other colored soldiers more and more menial jobs instead of military duty. The closest military task was guard duty which they had in addition to other work. They had no leisure time like the white soldiers.

"Do you like always being stuck in the kitchen?" Private Mosley asked Cathay one night.

Cathay thought a minute. "Well, I get out to drive the wood wagon some. And I guess the kitchen's better than fixing fences and telegraph wires."

"Yeah, I reckon you right. At least you get to eat better when you in the kitchen," Mosley said chuckling. "I know Sergeant Agee some upset because he was sent to work on the roads. He thought he be in charge-a something better since he be head of our platoon."

Cathay nodded. "You know them white officers ain't gonna give us nothing but road work and mending fences and laying bricks; just work fixing up this broken down place. I'm lucky because I knew cooking before I joined up. Even then I don't do no cooking in the kitchen. Just always cleaning and taking out garbage."

Mosley turned to leave. "Well, I better be getting off. I'm on patrol 'til the moon gets high. First they make me shoe horses during the day, horses they don't let me ride. Then I gotta go do guard duty at night, missing a good night's sleep on top."

Cathay shook her head as she watched Ben Mosley jog away. She was surprised to hear him complain. He usually griped less than most of the soldiers in Company A. That was why she didn't mind talking with him. She liked having someone she could talk to since she missed being with Henry and Jasper. She felt a longing for the kind of companionship a woman wants with a man.

Wonder if I'll ever decide to settle down and marry. I bet Ben Mosley make somebody a good husband one day.

However, she knew she would have to be ever cautious during her conversations with Mosley. His friendship could turn out to be disastrous to her as a soldier. And especially since she wasn't ready to quit the military.

* * *

A few days later, some of the soldiers in Company A crowded around the flagpole on the parade ground. They were all talking at once in angry voices. Sergeant Thornton Reaves, one of the group's leaders, stomped back and forth in front of them. Private Cathay approached the assembly to find out what was causing the ruckus.

"Mattie say she didn't steal money from Lieutenant Leggett's room," Cathay heard Sergeant Reaves shout. "She say the lieutenant just accused her because she his servant and because she colored. Could-a been anybody."

Another soldier chimed in. "He got no right to tell that Lieutenant Sweet to put Maggie off the fort. He needs to investigate first."

Reaves slammed his fist into his hand. "We can't stand for this foolishness."

The soldiers continued grumbling and Cathay could see they were working themselves up to fight. More soldiers from the company joined the group. Cathay knew they weren't supposed to gather like that without permission, but she was devoted to her platoon. She always did her work well and never got into trouble. But if her companions had been wronged, Private William Cathay wanted to stand with them.

The soldiers in Company A liked Mattie, one of the laundresses. She was also a maid to the white Lieutenant Leggett. When not tending to her duties, Mattie joked and teased the soldiers and they felt like she was one of them. Lieutenant Leggett resented Mattie's popularity. He also didn't like the fact that Mattie bragged about her brother who was one of the elite Buffalo Soldier 10th Cavalry. He preferred to treat all the colored people on the fort as though they were still slaves.

Cathay liked Mattie, too. Since Cathay's cousin, Jasper, was also a member of the 10th Cavalry, Mattie often shared news about the regiment's adventures. Company A and Cathay hated to see something bad happen to Mattie. They knew it would be wrong to send a defenseless woman out into the wilderness alone without any protection, if that was what Leggett had ordered.

Just then Lieutenant Sweet strode up to the group of soldiers. "You men break up this crowd. You know better than to gather without permission."

No one moved. The soldiers glared at Sweet defiantly.

The officer put his hands on his hips. He was not as racist as Lieutenant Leggett, so was not used to seeing this kind of contempt from the colored soldiers. Nor was he used to having his orders defied.

"I guess you know if you don't break up this group, you'll be charged with mutiny," he shouted. "You'll all be punished." Lieutenant Sweet waited a few minutes to see if the group would disperse. When no one moved he realized he was outnumbered. Sweet turned around and marched away to report the incident to Captain Clarke.

The soldiers milled about a few minutes longer until they saw Captain Clarke coming toward the parade ground. Not wanting to defy the captain, who always treated the company with respect, the crowd broke up and one by one they wandered back to their various duties. Cathay wondered what punishment there would be, if any.

Later that night, Sergeant Reaves and Sergeant Sam Allen met with Company A in their quarters. "We need to make sure we stay armed all the time," said Allen. "No telling what these officers gonna do now we showed them we ain't gonna act like slaves."

"Maybe we need to tell Captain Clarke what happened," said one of the soldiers. Several others shook their heads.

"Naw," said Reaves. "We just handle this problem ourselves."

The rest, including Private William Cathay, nodded in agreement.

CHAPTER 41

For several days Private Cathay worked in the kitchen with her rifle standing in the corner. The men in Company A worked at their jobs armed with muskets and rifles also. As Lieutenants Leggett and Sweet continued to assign the platoon the toughest and dirtiest duties on the post, the atmosphere became more and more tense. The officers had searched Mattie and her quarters and found nothing belonging to Leggett. Meanwhile, the order still stood for Mattie to be banished into the wilderness away from the fort. The Buffalo Soldiers of Company A were determined not to let that happen. Sergeants Reaves and Allen privately assigned platoon members to watch Mattie's quarters around the clock. They vowed to protect her, especially since she said she was innocent. Cathay took her turn watching Mattie's place just like the others in the platoon.

One night, a week after the gathering at the flagpole, she lay curled up on guard behind the laundress quarters where Mattie stayed. Cathay heard a commotion toward the front of the cabin.

Four white soldiers arrived with a wagon to escort Mattie to the Fort Cummings gate. It was early in the morning and the sun was just appearing over the eastern horizon. Few occupants at the fort were stirring. The officers intended to send Mattie away before the Buffalo Soldiers arose.

Cathay sprang into action and hurried to the platoon compound to notify Sergeant Reaves, while Mattie gathered up her belongings. Reaves rounded up the members of Company A.

At the gate, the white soldiers met Cathay and about thirty other members of her platoon. The Buffalo Soldiers drew their muskets or rifles and cried, "Halt." Reaves and Allen overpowered the escort and forced them to leave the wagon. Then, with Mattie still in the wagon, they took her safely to friendly settlers away from the fort.

When the escorts informed Captain Clarke of the platoon members' action, he ordered all the Buffalo Soldiers confined to quarters. Because of their attack on the escorts, Sergeants Reaves and Allen were immediately placed under arrest and taken to the guardhouse when they returned.

Cathay waited anxiously thinking someone would come to arrest her, but Captain Clarke did not know how many of Company A were involved. So he only charged Reaves and Allen as the ringleaders. He also charged the seven other Buffalo Soldiers who assisted in Mattie's escape with mutiny. The officers ordered that they all be placed in the Fort Cummings guardhouse.

Later, they took Reaves and Allen to Fort Selden near the Texas border for a court martial. The seven other soldiers remained in the guardhouse for several weeks. Although the Captain confined the rest of the regiment to the fort, they were not tried for anything. Cathay felt sad about what happened to Reaves and Allen and the soldiers who helped Mattie. But she was relieved that her record as a good soldier had not been tarnished.

* * *

Private William Cathay was not performing the duties she had expected in the military. *I'm not fighting Indians or protecting settlers. I'm not guarding railroad workers laying tracks. I'm doing guard duty, but that's just walking up and down outside this fort every day. I'm doing the same kinda work I did before I joined this here army. I'm not even doing no cooking. We not even seeing no more Indians.* Cathay was beginning to feel discontented being a soldier.

Also, officers punished the Buffalo Soldiers more and more. After the Mattie issue, they paid dearly for the least little infraction of rules. Lieutenant Leggett punished men if they didn't say "sir" when spoken to. He claimed the men spoke to him rudely and did not obey orders. Lieutenant Sweet chastised a soldier for wearing a torn uniform or would say the soldiers' uniforms were not worn properly. Since the Buffalo Soldiers' uniforms were those cast off from white soldiers and were usually shabby and ill fitting when they received them, this happened often. Once Sweet claimed he found Private Cathay's musket dirty right after she had cleaned it. He made her clean it again.

Whippings were common reminders of the harsh life the Buffalo Soldiers had spent as slaves. The officers' favorite punishment for some was to make them stand on kegs in the center of the fort for hours. The white officers hoped this would be humiliating and show what little respect they had for the colored soldiers. Seeing all of these injustices, Cathay wondered if it wasn't time for her to leave the service. While army life was not what she expected it to be, it had showed her that she had the strength to survive many hardships.

What would have happened if the Union soldiers had not taken her from her mama? Would she have been able to learn all the things she did with the army? Cathay never wanted to cook no matter how much her mama had insisted. But her mama's words came back to her. *There's no future here for you. You can make yourself useful just like you been doing here with me.*

And she had been useful. Cathay had learned to cook and to nurse and to drill and to manage her weapons. She had chopped trees, hauled wood, mended fences and stood guard duty. She had figured out how to fool the soldiers too. No one had discovered Private William Cathay's real gender. Most of all she did not have to depend on others to decide what her life would be like.

Mama and Jasper would be proud of me.

While Cathay had wanted to prove she was as capable as any of the male soldiers, she proved much more to herself. She didn't need the army any more. She had signed up for three years, but Cathay decided to end her service with the army sooner. Service with the Buffalo Soldiers no longer held any excitement or charm.

Should I get out without showing I'm a woman? Or should I let the officers and platoon members know that a woman can be just as able as any man in the military?

A few more weeks would give her time to decide. Private Cathay did not count on another incident determining her decision.

CHAPTER 42

Cathay was working near the south entrance of Fort Cummings. Since all of Company A had been confined to the fort, they had not been allowed on wood patrol after the mutiny. She and Private Ben Mosley were replacing the rusty hinges on the wooden stockade gate. She felt friendly toward Mosley ever since he had saved her from drowning in the Rio Grande. He never asked her about that incident. If he suspected she was a woman, he never mentioned it. Also, he was not a troublemaker like some others in her platoon.

"What do you think will happen to Reaves and Allen?" Cathay asked Mosley. He, Cathay, and the remaining members of the platoon awaited word of results from Fort Selden and the court martial of Reaves and Allen.

"I don't know," said Ben. "I only hope they aren't sentenced to a firing squad. Or hanged. No telling what the courts will cook up for us colored soldiers."

Cathay wanted to tell Ben Mosley about her thoughts of leaving the army, but didn't know how without revealing that she was a woman. As she pondered over her decision, they received word to report to the Fort Cummings command office. There they met Sergeant Agee and a group of other soldiers.

Special orders had come from the New Mexico military command at Santa Fe. The orders demanded that soldiers go north from Fort Cummings and join other New Mexico troops from Fort Bayard and Fort Craig to destroy a major Apache village in the Black Range Mountains.

The Apache Indians surrounding Fort Bayard were tough and aggressive. They resented the settlement of their lands by white people; Spanish from Mexico and American settlers from the eastern states. They especially resented the soldiers who came to protect the intruding settlers. Cathay remembered the Indians that she had encountered when she served on wood patrol. They did not seem to be herders or farmers like their counterparts in other areas of the country. They appeared to be hunters and fighters. She had been told those Apaches made their homes in the mountains and desert canyons.

Captain Clarke and other officers were away at Fort Selden attending the court martial of the Company A mutineers when the orders came. Major Merriam had left Fort Cummings to return to Fort Bayard and had taken several platoons with him. All those left were Cathay and the remainder of Company A, a couple of other companies, and a few Buffalo Soldier cavalrymen.

The acting Fort Cummings commander was reluctant to send troops from an already sparse force of soldiers. However, when the post commander read the orders, he thought sending Company A might be a good way to rid the fort of what he considered a troublesome platoon. He ordered Sergeant Agee to select twenty-five members of Company A to join the campaign. Cathay noted the ones assigned were all hard working soldiers. She was one of them.

"Now what?" muttered Private Mosley as he threw a few belongings and a canteen into his haversack.

Cathay busied herself strapping her cartridge pouch to her belt and checking her musket. She hunched her shoulders and heaved a big sigh in response.

"Looks like we be moving again," she said. She knew her plans to leave the army had to be postponed if she was assigned to a special campaign. *This might be a way I can at least show how good I am at doing some real soldiering,* she thought.

As Private William Cathay and her companions took their places in formation, Sergeant Agee explained their mission.

"We gonna join some troops from Fort Bayard and Fort Craig. They want us to get rid of Apaches that been raiding Fort Bayard. They say they need us 'cause we infantry fighters. Cavalry ain't no good because horses too hard to ride in those canyons and mountains. We infantry, we gotta go."

CHAPTER 43

And who did Cathay see at the head of the platoon? The hated Lieutenant Leggett, who had ordered Mattie Merritt's expulsion, would head the campaign. In the absence of Captain Clarke, the acting post commander had to select an experienced officer to lead the group. He decided Leggett, an outstanding Civil War officer and leader of various Indian offensives, would be the best officer in charge.

It was winter. A disgruntled Leggett wasn't pleased to have to venture north on a campaign and especially with a platoon that he disliked and he knew disliked him.

Although in southern New Mexico, the higher elevation of Fort Bayard created a colder and windier climate than that in the desert-like Fort Cummings. Cathay remembered the cold weather of northern New Mexico and she and her platoon comrades dressed as warmly as they could in their woolen uniforms and snug neckerchiefs. Their kepis covered their heads over their neckerchiefs and they pulled their jacket collars up to try to cover their ears. Unhappy about having to move again, still Cathay felt the Fort Bayard campaign would prove that the members of Company A were not troublemakers, but good soldiers.

Cathay had decided to quit the military and use her former illnesses as the reason. But since she had been selected as one of the soldiers chosen for the campaign, she decided to show her fortitude as a dedicated member of her platoon one more time.

The platoon left Fort Cummings shortly after receiving the orders from Sergeant Agee. With Lieutenant Leggett in the lead, Cathay and Company A marched northward across the barren winter desert. They moved into the mountainous country surrounded by high, snow-covered peaks. Arriving at the icy creeks that ran off from the Rio Grande River, Cathay shivered more from memory than from the cold. As she waded through the creeks, she recalled her near drowning when crossing the Rio Grande on the way to Fort Cummings. Her ears still throbbed whenever she got a cold or encountered bad weather.

The group trudged with wet feet in wet socks in wet shoes farther and farther north. Cathay did not know what they were going to face when they arrived at their meeting with the Fort Bayard forces. As she marched alongside Private Mosley, she wondered about their assignment. A part of Cathay reasoned how much the Indians' situation was like the slaves' plight had been.

"Don't know why we gotta go destroy that Apache village. There must be women and children up there as well as braves. Seem like those peoples fighting to keep their freedom just like we wanted ours back aways."

"Yeah, and we wasn't free like they is," said Mosley. "They got even more reason to fight. Guess the army want them to be slaves instead-a us."

As they neared the canyon in Apache territory, Cathay cast wary looks at the steep walls that could easily hide their attackers and put the platoon in danger of an ambush.

Lieutenant Leggett thought the same thing. His experience told him that any canyon could be a death trap to his men. He decided to wait for the troops from Forts Bayard and Craig before entering the canyon. He ordered Cathay and the other soldiers in the platoon to make camp at the base of the frosty, tree-covered mountains.

Cathay wanted to make a fire to warm herself, but Lieutenant Leggett ordered the soldiers not to light fires that would reveal their presence. The mouth of the canyon loomed ominously in the dark before the cold, weary Buffalo Soldiers. Cathay did not get much sleep. She was continually on guard for expected attacks from Apaches that she imagined might swoop down on the small, unsuspecting platoon at any moment.

Days passed in discomfort, but the nights were the worst. The temperature always dropped sharply at night, making the already cold weather more severe and the soldiers even more miserable.

As the small contingent from Company A awaited the arrival of the Fort Bayard and Fort Craig platoons, food rations grew low and hunger added to the soldiers' misery. Finally, Lieutenant Leggett decided the promised additional troops would not be coming. He ordered his company back to Fort Cummings, returning by the same route.

Cathay and her companions were relieved when ordered to head back to Fort Cummings, but the return was as difficult as the forward march. A huge blizzard and bitter winds accompanied their retreat. Cathay's feet that were wet before, became frostbitten and numb. She could not cover her ears sufficiently. Her eyelashes froze and, at times, she couldn't feel her face. She could never remember being in such brutal weather.

As the worn and half frozen troops stumbled back to Fort Cummings, Cathay became definitely resolved to end her military career. *This gonna be my last campaign with this Buffalo Soldier Infantry.*

CHAPTER 44

After the severe wintry campaign, Private William Cathay's health began to deteriorate.

She appeared at the Fort Cummings Infirmary with a continual, raspy cough. Each time she entered the infirmary, Cathay wondered if the infirmary surgeon would discover her gender. Each time he came up with another diagnosis, but did not make her disrobe. When the infirmary surgeon realized Cathay had been coughing blood, he ordered her to be admitted. The surgeon said Cathay had pneumonia. But, after three days, the surgeon released Cathay from the infirmary. Her platoon chief once more assigned her to duty.

Since she had recently been in the infirmary in poor health, Cathay went back to work in the kitchen. The tasks were less strenuous than those outdoors.

"You lucky," commented Private Mosley. "You don't have no guard duty. We got patrol duty besides building that wall." He was referring to the latest Buffalo Soldier task, carrying stone from a quarry to build a wall around the Fort Cummings cemetery.

"I hope I gets rid-a this cough soon so's I can get back to workin' with my platoon," Cathay said. "Maybe soon."

But it wasn't long before Cathay returned to the infirmary again. Her feet continued to swell and her toes remained blue from frostbite. This time the surgeon said she had rheumatism. Her numb toes and blue feet caused the surgeon to say Cathay's frostbite had resulted in poor circulation. Again Cathay stayed three days.

Little by little Cathay began to regain her strength. Her cough lessened. Her rheumatism subsided. Her feet still continued to swell when she returned to guard duty where she had to stand for hours at a time. At least she didn't have to work on the wall.

After the unsuccessful winter campaign, the Buffalo Soldiers returned to wood patrols. Driving the mule-drawn wagon for the wood gathering detail allowed Cathay to stay off her feet. She still helped load the wood that the other soldiers cut. Not wanting to seem a loafer, she helped the men at whatever chore they had to perform.

Cathay knew it would soon be time to leave the army. Even though she knew she would lose her thirteen dollar-a-month salary, a medical discharge with a pension would give her money to live on until she could find work.

Every few days Private Cathay appeared at the infirmary. Her feet were still swollen. The pneumonia left her wheezing and often it was hard to breathe. Recurring rheumatism kept her sore and stiff. Her ears throbbed and she said she was going deaf from her fall in the Rio Grande and the winter campaign. The doctors ignored most of Cathay's complaints and didn't record any of them.

Meanwhile, trouble at Fort Bayard required reinforcements. Once again the entire Company A received orders to transfer. At Fort Bayard there were constant Indian raids. The Apaches stole livestock. Some of the patrols returned carrying fellow soldiers who had been killed with arrows. But Company A had received such poor treatment at Fort Cummings, the soldiers were only too happy to serve somewhere else.

Despite Cathay's poor physical condition, she welcomed the change. She hoped the summer weather would make the trek easier than it was during the winter campaign. She also hoped the warmer climate would help her rheumatism.

However, Fort Bayard with its higher elevation was as remote as Fort Cummings. Cathay struggled to keep up with the march. Her breath came in gasps. Her feet ached constantly. She and her company had to be continually aware of imminent Apache attacks.

Learning that Major Merriam was the commander of Fort Bayard encouraged Private Cathay. She respected Major Merriam as she did Captain Clarke. Captain Clarke was compassionate. Major Merriam was fair. Cathay decided Fort Bayard would be the right place to ask for her discharge from the military.

CHAPTER 45

While the soldiers of Company A hoped the new post would be as pleasant as Fort Union, conditions at Fort Bayard were entirely different. In many ways its location and desolate surroundings made conditions worse than that of Fort Cummings. Log huts with dirt roofs formed the buildings in the company's quarters. Doors and windows did not close properly, and centipedes, scorpions, and poisonous spiders crawled in through the cracks.

Contrary to Cathay's earlier reasoning, and despite the higher elevation, the broiling heat during the summer did not relieve Cathay's deteriorating health. Located near the southwestern border of Arizona, food and medical provisions remained low because supply depots were far away from the post.

Soon after arriving at Fort Bayard, Cathay once more landed in the infirmary. She complained of stabbing pains in her face and lower jaw especially along the front of her ear. Sometimes an eye twitched uncontrollably. At that time the fort doctors said she had neuralgia, a disease of the nervous system.

Cathay spent more than a month in the infirmary. Doctors treated her with various salves and poultices applied to her face. They gave her morphine-like pain killers. While the water from the area's natural springs was a refreshing part of her treatment, nothing helped her morale. Private Cathay was determined to leave the military.

* * *

Tall, slender Private William Cathay entered the Fort Bayard infirmary office for the fifth time with multiple complaints.

The post doctor greeted Cathay with a sour expression. He pulled out her medical record and skimmed through the pages of the little information on file.

"You've been in and out of this infirmary five times," the doctor snapped. "First one thing and then another is always wrong with you. There are others that have the same complaints and don't seem to linger on their illnesses like you do."

"Yes, sir, Lieutenant, sir. I know. But now I really think the deafness in my ears is worse. You remember it come from swimming in the river before we got to Fort Cummings. I can't hear the sergeant's orders. Marching mostly makes my legs give out, especially since I ain't got no feeling in my feet."

"I'm tired of having to come up with diagnoses for all your complaints," the post surgeon told Cathay. He stared at her for a long time. Then he shook his head in disgust. "Go on to the back so I can check you again. This is the last time I'm going to be bothered. Next time I'm going to order that you be discharged from the army." He turned away and gathered up her papers as Cathay limped back to the examination room.

The doctor did not see the twinkle in her eyes as the corners of Cathay's mouth turned up in a smirk. Now she had heard the magic word.

Discharge.

Private William Cathay would not wait for the next visit. She would make sure the doctor discovered her startling, well-kept secret when he examined her. And she was sure it would result in exactly what she wanted.

A discharge.

ARMY OF THE UNITED STATES.

CERTIFICATE

OF DISABILITY   FOR DISCHARGE

William Cathay, a *private*, of Captain *Clarke*
Company, (*a*) of the *Thirty Eighth* Regiment of the United States
Infantry was enlisted by *Maj. Merriam* of
the *38th* Regiment of *Infantry* at *Saint Louis Mo.*
on the *15th* day of *November*, 186*6*, to serve *3* years; he was born
in *Independence* in the State of *Missouri*, is *24*
years of age, *5* feet *9* inches high, *Black* complexion, *Black* eyes,
Black hair, and by occupation when enlisted a *Cook*. During the last two
months said soldier has been unfit for duty *60* days.* *This soldier has been under my
command since May 20th 1867. At that time he was doing Garrison
Duty at Fort Harker Kansas. He has there ever has been since feeble both
physically and mentally and much of the time quite unfit for duty. The
origin of this infirmities is unknown to me.*

STATION *Fort Bayard N. M.*
DATE: *August 4th 1868*

Charles E. Clarke
Capt. 38th Inf. Bvt. Maj. USA
Commanding Company.

I CERTIFY, that I have carefully examined the said *William Cathay Private*
of Captain *Charles E. Clarke* (*a*) Company, and find him incapable of performing the duties of a
soldier because of † *a scrofulous and feeble habit. He is continually
on sick report without benefit. He is unable to do military
duty and is unfit for any service involving the least exer-
tion. This condition dates prior to enlistment.*
Disability ½

D. S. Huntington
Bvt. Lt. Col. USA Surgeon USA

DISCHARGED, this *Fourteenth* day of *October*, 186*8*, *at*
Fort Bayard NM

Clifford
Lt. 38 Inf
Commanding the Reg't.

The Soldier desires to be addressed at
Town *Alton* county *Madison* State *Illinois*

*See Note 1 on the back of this.   † See Note 3 on the back of this.

[A. G. O., No. 100 & 121—First.]   [DUPLICATE.]

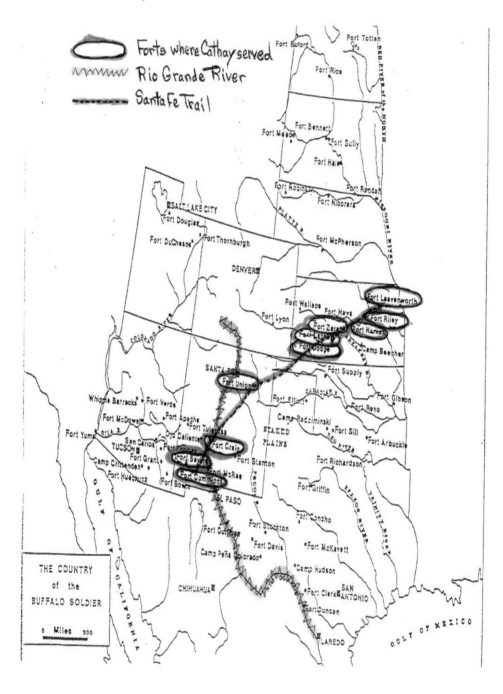

AFTERWORD

When the members of her platoon found out she was a woman, Cathay said the men treated her badly. They claimed she was always sick because she was a weakling woman. Perhaps it was not because Cathay wasn't a loyal member of their platoon. They knew she had done the same tasks they did, and handled her weapons even better than some. The men were irate when they realized how thoroughly they had been deceived. *And by a woman.*

Cathay Williams received an honorable discharge as William Cathay from Fort Bayard, New Mexico. She returned to Fort Union where she had been happiest. She worked as a cook for one of the colonels at the fort for two years. Later, Cathay went to Trinidad, Colorado where there was a thriving community of former African-American slaves. A journalist from the St. Louis Daily Times heard of a black woman who served in the regular army as a man. He sought Cathay out for an interview and published an article about her in the January 2, 1876 St. Louis Daily Times.

Another article in the January 21, 1890 issue of the Pueblo, Colorado Daily Chieftain described a Catherine

Williams who worked at housecleaning and washing. The Daily Times journalist also referred to Cathay as Kate. It is believed the two women were the same.

Besides military documents, the Daily Times article is believed to be the only known personal record of Cathay's life.

Historical documents show Cathay Williams being denied the disability pension for which she applied. When examined for the pension, the doctor in Trinidad, who was an employee of the Pension Bureau, noted several of Cathay's toes had been amputated. Since he did not state a reason for the amputation, the Pension Board rejected Cathay's claim on the basis that no proof of frostbite caused amputation of her toes. The army medical staff never recorded the frostbite. The Board also said she could not claim deafness due to the Rio Grande experience because she could hear the pension doctor talking to her.

Her rejection could have been because she was a woman and not legally a member of the armed services. That claim was not made. Cathay had documentation that she received an honorable discharge from the army. The army would have had to admit it had been duped.

Cathay William's date and place of death and burial are unknown at the time of this writing.

Pension Papers

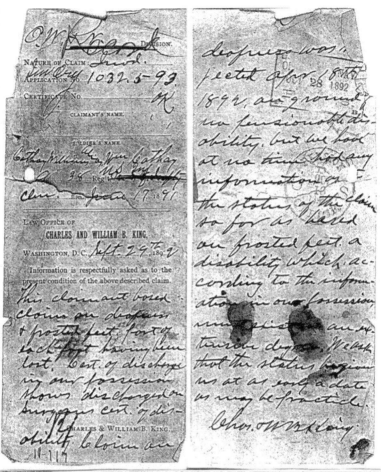

RESOURCES

BUFFALO SOLDIERS
1. Buffalo Soldiers, The A Historical Review
   www.sru.edu/depts./scc/collaborate/pages/buffalo/
   polk.html
2. Dixon, David *Campaigning with the Buffalo Soldiers*
   www.sru.edu/depts./scc/buffalo/campaigning-
   html
3. Field, Ron *Buffalo Soldiers 1866-91,* Osprey Publishing, 2008
4. Leckie, William H, *The Buffalo Soldiers-A Narrative of the Negro Cavalry in   the West,* University of Oklahoma Press, 1999
5. McCrae, Bennie J., Jr. *Buffalo Soldiers on the Western Frontier,* Lest We Forget, LWF Publications, 1994
6. McDermott, John D. *A Guide to the Indian Wars of the West,* University of Nebraska Press, 1998
7. Negro in the Regular Army, The
   www.emedia.netlibrary.com/nlreader
8. Recipe for Hard Tack Crackers
   www.fortunecity.com
9. Schubert, Frank N. *Voices of the Buffalo Soldiers,* University of New Mexico Press, 2003

RESOURCES continued

CATHAY WILLIAMS

1. Blanton, DeAnne, 1992, Excerpt: "Quarterly report on Women and the Military" MINERVA Vol.X, numbers 3&4, Fall/Winter, pp.1-12
2. Cathay Williams, Female Buffalo Soldier www.shider.com/history/
3. Cox, Major W. Article, *Female Buffalo Soldier lived Life of Excitement and Inspiration* - www.majorcox.com/columns/buffalo.htm - Permission granted by Major Cox
4. Discharge Paper – Record group 15, Record of Department of Veteran Affairs, Pension Application file SO1032593
5. Enlistment Papers – December 1866-October 1868, Record group 94, Record of Adjutant General Office, Regular Army enlistment paper, Cathey Williams
6. Excerpt from *Buffalo Soldiers and Indian Wars,* www.buffalosoldier.net
7. Female Buffalo Soldier: The Legend www.buffalosoldiersmonument.com
8. Savage, Cynthia, 1997 Oral presentation, "Black Woman Soldier", by Cynthia Savage to West Texas Historical Society
9. Tucker, Phillip Thomas, 2002 *Cathay Williams – from Slave to Female Buffalo Soldier,* - permission granted from Maria Metzler, Stackpole Books, publisher Ibid, Review of book www.cw-book-news.com, pac.lib.ci.phoenix.az.us

RESOURCES continued

CIVIL WAR

1. *American Heritage Picture History of the Civil War,* 1961, American Heritage Publishing Company, Inc. NY
2. Battle of Pea Ridge – General Samuel R. Curtis en.wikipedia.org/wiki/Battle_of_Pea_Ridge
3. Benton,WilliamPlummer1828 – 1867,
4. www.indianainthecivilwar.com/hoosier
5. Emancipation Proclamation Transcript, U.S. National Archives, www.archives.gov
6. Hansen, Harry, 2002, *The Civil War, A History.* Penguin Books, NY publisher
7. A Brief Biography of General Philip Henry Sheridan, compiled by Bob Miller, Somerset, Ohio www.netpluscom.com/Npchs/Sheridan.htm

SLAVERY

1. Antbellum Slavery: Plantation Slave Life www.cghs.dade.k12.fl.us/slavery/antebellum
2. Missouri Plantations: An Introduction www.rootsweb.com

RESOURCES continued

MISCELLANEOUS
    1. Apache Clothing
       www.cryatalinks.com/apache.html
    2. Encarta Encyclopedia, Lives on Santa
       Fe Trail, www.Encarta.msn.com
    3. Encarta Encyclopedia, New Mexico,
       Geography, Animal & Plant Life,
       Rivers & Lakes
       www.encarta.msn.com
    4. Fort Craig www.over-
       land.com/fortcraig
    5. Fort Harker www.stjohnlinks.net
    6. Fort Union
       www.nps.gov/foun/adhi1.htm
    7. Jefferson Barracks
       www.missouricivilwarmuseum.org
    8. Old West Forts & Towns www.over-
       land.com/westfort.html
    9. Quarantine Hospital–Early St. Louis
       Hospitals
       http://genealogyinstlouis.accessgeneol
       ogy.net
   10. Smallpox
       www.bt.cdc.gov/agent/smallpox
          Merck Manual of Medical
       Information 2nd Home Ed (2003)
          Taber's Cyclopedic Medical
       Dictionary Ed. 20 (2005)
   11. Wadsworth, Ginger 1993 *Along the
       Santa Fe Trail* (Marion Russell Story),
       Albert Whitman, NY publisher

RESOURCES continued

INTERVIEWS
1. Cox, Wade, Union Army Civil War re-enactor and historian, personal interview and research material, Fort Verde, AZ
2. Hayes, Roland, Buffalo Soldier Indian War re-enactor and historian, personal interview and research material, Newtown Square, PA
3. Madison, Donna, Buffalo Soldier researcher, Kansas City, MO, Telephone interview
4. Sanchez, Roger, Raton Museum Curator, Raton, NM, Telephone interview

NOTES

The story is fictional but the following characters were real persons:

Colonel William Plummer Benton
Captain Charles E. Clarke
Brig. General Samuel E. Curtis
William & Elizabeth Johnson
Second Lt Henry F. Leggett
Major Henry Merriam
General Philip Henry Sheridan
Lt. William E. Sweet
Martha Williams, Cathay's mother

The forts were actual places along the Santa Fe Trail and in New Mexico.